DON'T JUST TAKE
EVEN PROFESSIO
LOVE BAD KITTY.

★ "In this heavily illustrated chapter book loaded with science facts and plenty of laughs, [Bad Kitty] proves once again she's a force to be reckoned with. Multiple copies are a must." —*Kirkus Reviews*, Starred Review

"This follow-up to *Bad Kitty* pairs Bruel's witty asides and spastic, tongue-in-cheek commentaries with more high-energy cartoon illustrations. . . . Whether they prefer cats or dogs, young and reluctant readers will get plenty of laughs from this comic and informative chapter book." —*Booklist*

"Bruel's zany illustrations incorporate numerous perspectives that heighten the humor." —*School Library Journal*

BAD KITTY Gets a BATH

NICK BRUEL

SQUARE FISH

ROARING BROOK PRESS
New York

For Jules, Jenny, Kate, Halley, Julie,
and the rest of the Fabulous Feiffers.

An imprint of Macmillan Publishing Group, LLC

 Printed in the United States of America by
Lakeside Book Company, Harrisonburg, Virginia.
For information, address
Square Fish, 120 Broadway, New York, NY 10271.

Library of Congress Cataloging-in-Publication Data
Bruel, Nick.
Bad kitty gets a bath / Nick Bruel.
p. cm.
"A Neal Porter book."
Summary: Takes a humorous look at the way normal cats bathe, why it is inappropriate for humans to bathe that way, and the challenges of trying to give a cat a real bath with soap and water. Includes fun facts, glossary, and other information.
ISBN 978-0-312-58138-1
[1. Cats—Fiction. 2. Baths—Fiction. 3. Humorous stories.] I. Title.
PZ7.B82832Bag 2008 [E]—dc22 2008020296

Originally published in the United States by Roaring Brook Press
Square Fish logo designed by Filomena Tuosto
Book design by Jennifer Browne
First Square Fish Edition: 2009
mackids.com

ISBN 978-1-250-86481-9 (special edition)
1 3 5 7 9 10 8 6 4 2

AR: 3.7 / F&P: X / LEXILE: 650L

• CONTENTS •

As you read this book, you'll notice
that there's an * following some of the words.

Those words will be defined in the Glossary*
at the back of this book.

• INTRODUCTION •

This is how Kitty likes to clean herself.

She licks her leg.

She licks her tail.

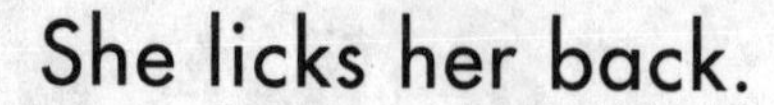

She licks her back.

And to clean her face, she licks her front paw and rubs it all over where her tongue can't reach.

LICK LICK LIC
ICK LICK LIC
LICK LICK LI
ICK LICK LIC
LICK LICK LI
ICK LICK LIC
LICK LICK LI
ICK LICK LIC
LICK LICK LI
ICK LICK LIC
LICK LICK LI

LICK LICK
LICK LICK
LICK LICK
LICK
LICK LICK
Sometimes, Kitty will do this for hours.

UNCLE MURRAY'S FUN FACTS

WHY DO CATS LICK THEMSELVES?

This is a close-up of Kitty's tongue. It is covered with hundreds of tiny fishhook-shaped barbs called "papillae.*" These barbs help her to comb her fur as she licks herself. Her tongue will also serve to collect any loose fur that she could swallow.

Papillae are partly composed of fibrous protein called keratin. Do you know what else is made of keratin? *Your fingernails!*

HOLY SALAMI! THAT GOOFY CAT'S GOT HUNDREDS OF TINY FINGERNAILS ON HER TONGUE!

Kitty has to be careful. Sometimes, if she licks her fur too much, she can develop a HAIR BALL.

Hair balls form in Kitty's stomach when she swallows too much fur.

Sometimes, the only way to get rid of that hair ball is to cough it up.

Coughing up
a hair ball isn't
always easy.

They can be
stubborn.

And sometimes
those hair balls
can be pretty
darn big.

WARNING!

You should NEVER clean yourself
the same way as Kitty!

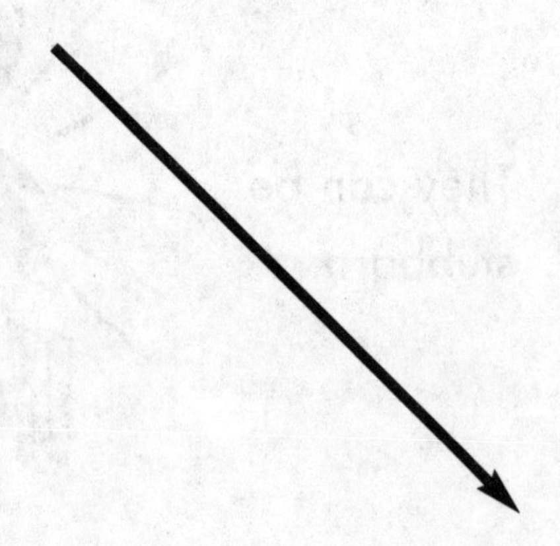

DAILY NOOZ

KID SENT HOME FOR BAD BREATH—ALL OVER BODY

SCHOOL EVACUATED

"I forgot that I ate a garlic and egg pizza for lunch," said the oy, seen here in his picture walking ome and wishing remain anony-ous.

"Well, I saw my cat cleaning herself with her tongue," said the child. "So I thought to my-self, 'Gee, that looks like it could work on me, too!'"

Officials predict that the school will be re-opened in about a week once health officials have dealt

"We tried soak-ing the child in a solution made of toothpaste and mouthwash," said Principal Sarah Bellum. "But it just helped a little. We can only hope that this in-cident served as

So, this is how Kitty *USUALLY* cleans herself.

BUT . . .

Sometimes . . .

every now and then . . .

Kitty needs . . .

a real . . .

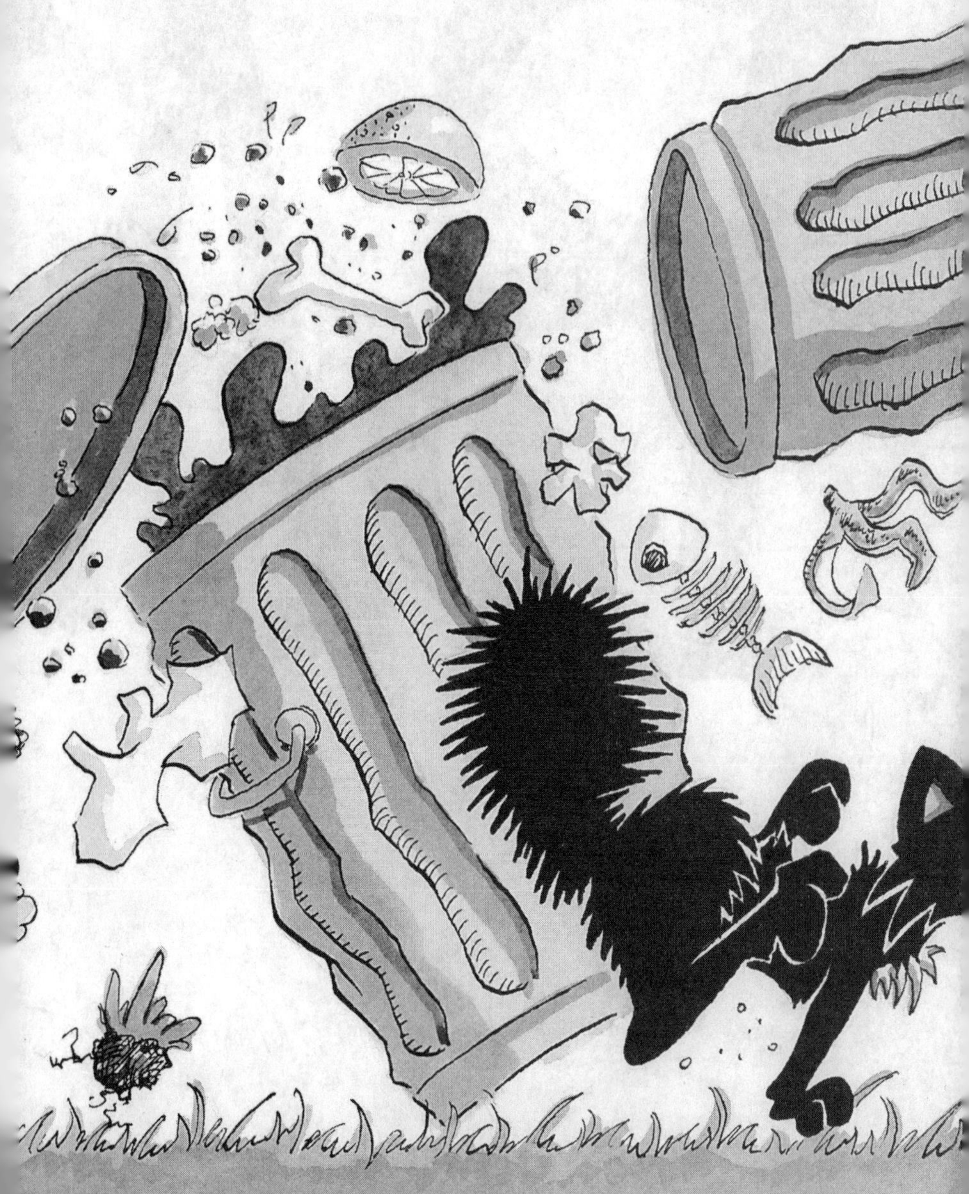

BA

I'H*

• CHAPTER ONE •

PREPARING KITTY'S BATH

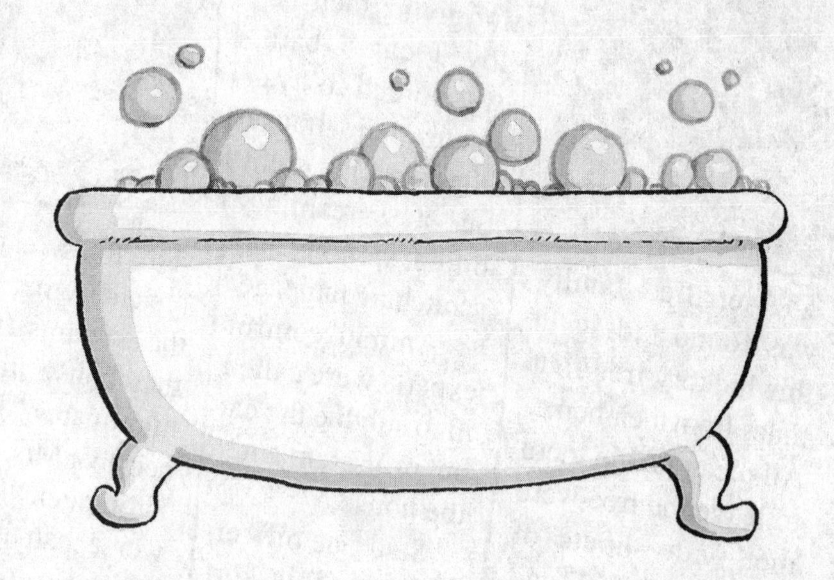

Do you remember the last time you tried to give Kitty a bath?

DAILY NOOZ

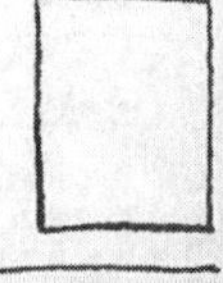

ENTIRE FAMILY FLEES FOR LIFE

The terrified family was found hiding in this hickory tree four miles from their home. All pleas asking them to leave the tree were met with shouts of "Eek," "Yipes," and "This is worse than when we ran out of food for the kitty."

The grisly story began when a local family, unprepared for giving their beloved cat a bath, was forced to evacuate their house after the kitty went on a screaming, biting, spitting, and scratching rampage.

Animal control experts were called in to subdue the cat but refused to enter the house.

Said one officer, "We see this sort of thing every time someone tries to give a cat a bath.

"Oh, the screams! I shall remember the screams from that house in my nightmares," sai neighbor Mrs. Edn Kroninger. "It wa worse than the da they ran out food for the kit I almost mov out of the nei

BE PREPARED.

The first lesson that all cat owners must learn is that . . .

CATS HATE BATHS

For your own safety, please repeat this to yourself four thousand eight hundred ninety-three times.

It's not that cats don't *like* baths. It's not that cats have a difficult relationship with baths. It's not that cats chose not to vote for baths in the last election. It's not that cats would rather choose vanilla over baths. It's not that cats neglect to send baths a card on their birthdays. It's not that cats pick baths last when choosing sides for a kick ball game. It's not that cats think about baths in the same way a fire hydrant thinks about dogs. It's not that cats look at baths in the same way that a vegetarian looks at ten pounds of raw liver. It's not that cats once bought baths an awesome present that cost an entire month's allowance, and then baths didn't even have the decency to say "thank you."

It's simply that . . .

CATS HATE BATHS!

Think about it this way . . .

UNCLE MURRAY'S FUN FACTS

HOW SHOULD I KNOW?

WHY DO CATS HATE BATHS?

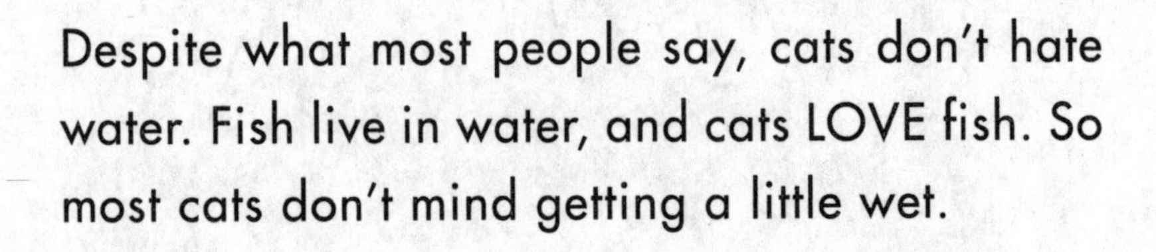

Despite what most people say, cats don't hate water. Fish live in water, and cats LOVE fish. So most cats don't mind getting a little wet.

But cats do HATE baths. That's because cats only like to get wet when they're the ones in control, when they choose to get wet. If someone else has decided to make them wet, they HATE it.

And if a cat *has* to get wet, the water had better be warm.

A cat's fur is very good at keeping her warm, but not so good at keeping her dry. So if a cat gets wet in cold weather, that poor cat will have a hard time getting warm again. And that poor cat can catch a bad cold.

So, cats should always be bathed in warm (NOT HOT) water.

ME, I LIKE TO SHOWER IN THE MORNING WHILE I SING OLD SHOW TUNES LIKE "SOMEWHERE OVER THE RAINBOW" . . .!

Cats hate showers, too. And they rarely sing old show tunes.

Now that you understand that cats hate baths (you will be tested), you will find it much easier to prepare Kitty's bath BEFORE putting her in it.

The following are some of the items you will need for Kitty's bath:

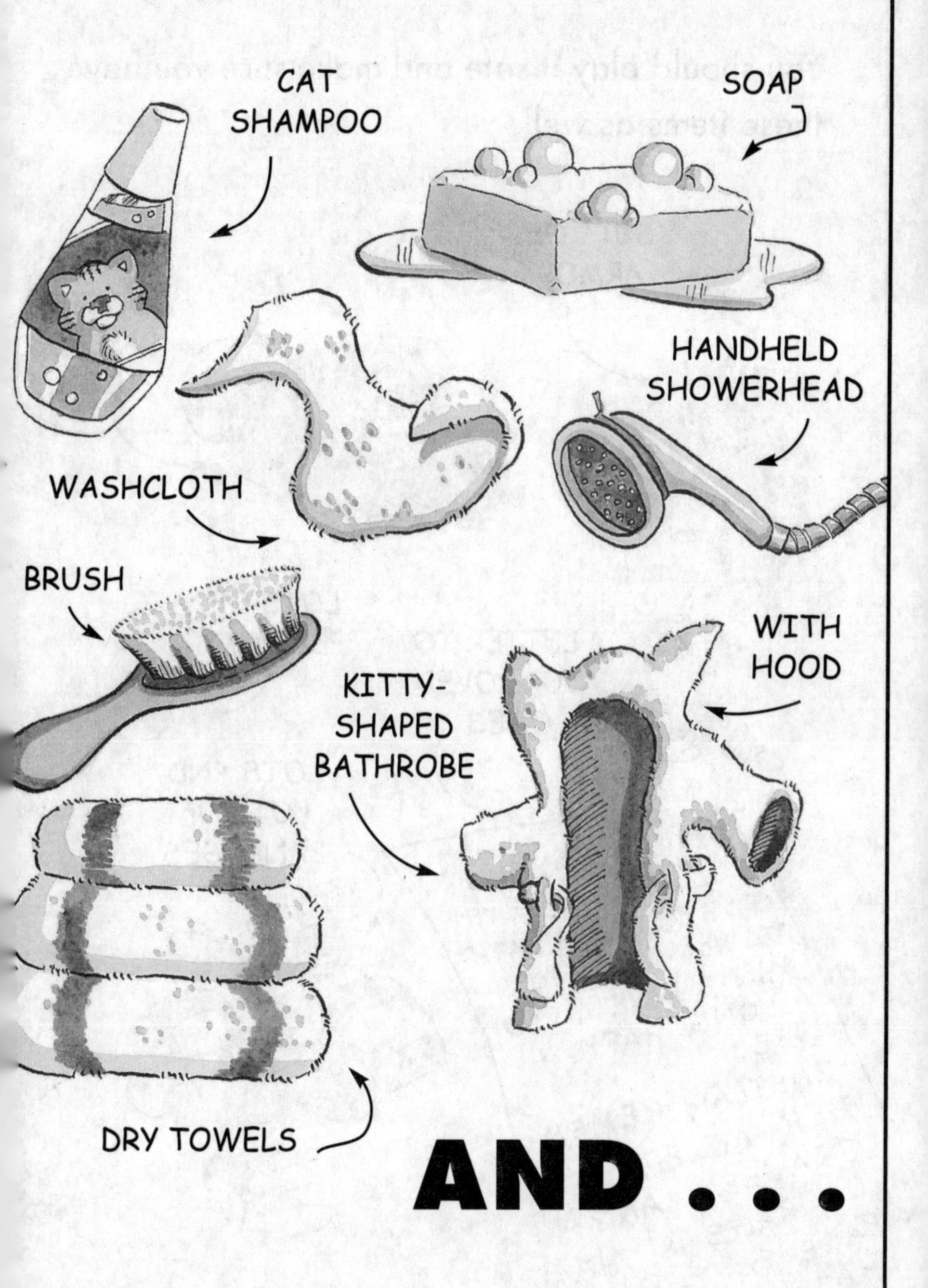
CAT SHAMPOO
SOAP
HANDHELD SHOWERHEAD
WASHCLOTH
BRUSH
WITH HOOD
KITTY-SHAPED BATHROBE
DRY TOWELS

AND . . .

You should play it safe and make sure you have these items as well.

SUIT OF ARMOR
YOUR DOCTOR ON SPEED DIAL
LOTS OF PLASMA*
A LETTER TO YOUR LOVED ONES
LOTS AND LOTS OF BANDAGES
DEAR FAMILY,
I AM GOING TO GIVE KITTY A BATH. DO NOT CRY FOR ME. I HAVE LIVED A LONG, HAPPY LIFE.
INSTEAD, REMEMBER ME FOR MY BRAVERY AND COURAGE IN THE FACE OF GIVING THAT CAT A BATH

CLEAN UNDERWEAR (BECAUSE STRESSFUL SITUATIONS CAN CAUSE "ACCIDENTS")

PLANE TICKETS AND A MAP TO YOUR AUNT PAULINE'S HOUSE WHERE YOU CAN HIDE WHEN THIS IS OVER

A SCRATCHING POST MADE TO LOOK LIKE YOU THAT MIGHT (BUT PROBABLY WON'T) FOOL KITTY

AN AMBULANCE IN YOUR DRIVEWAY WITH THE ENGINE RUNNING

And, of course, the last thing you'll need before giving Kitty a bath will be Kitty herself.

But try not to say that out loud.

QUICK QUIZ

FILL IN THE BLANKS.

CATS ______________

A) LOVE BATHS.

B) LIKE BATHS.

C) HATE BATHS.

D) ARE SMALL, FLIGHTLESS, DOMESTIC FOWL EASILY RECOGNIZED BY THEIR COMBS AND WATTLES* THAT CAN LAY AS MANY AS 250 EGGS A YEAR.

ANSWER: The correct answer is C. If you answered anything other than C, please reread Chapter One 753 more times or until you are saying "Cats Hate Baths" out loud in your sleep. If you answered D, please go immediately to an eye doctor, because the animal in your home that you think is a cat is really a chicken.

• CHAPTER TWO •

FINDING KITTY

Now's the hard part.

The bath is ready, but Kitty is not. In fact, Kitty is nowhere to be found.

Is she in her litter box?

Is she under the sofa?*

Is she sitting on her favorite window ledge?

NOPE.

Is she sitting in her favorite chair?

NOPE.

Is she lying in your bed?

NOPE.

So where is Kitty?

Kitty's very good at hiding. So maybe the best step right now would be to think about where you found her all the other times she hid.

This is where she was hiding when you had to take her to the vet.*

This is where she was hiding when you had to brush her teeth.

This is where she was hiding when you had to give her medicine.

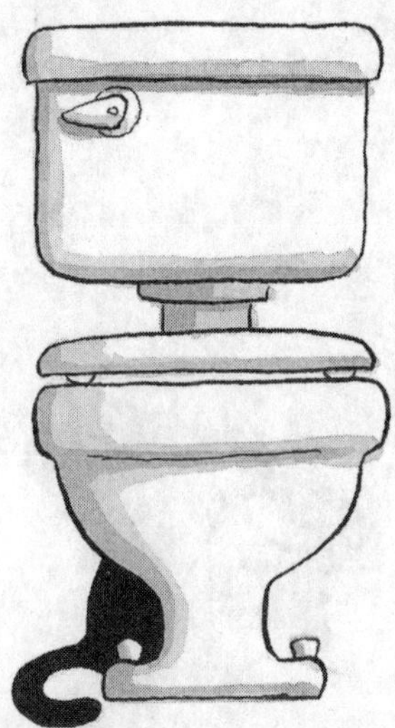

This is where she was hiding when you had to clip her nails.

This is where she was hiding when you told her to finish her veg-etables.*

There's Puppy!

Maybe Puppy knows where Kitty is hiding.

Hey, Puppy . . . Do you know where Kitty is hiding?

Hmmm . . . Maybe he doesn't know.

Hold on . . . Since when does Puppy have black fur? Puppy has never had black fur. So maybe that isn't Puppy at all. So who is it really? Hmmm . . .

IT'S KITTY IN DISGUISE!

GET HER!

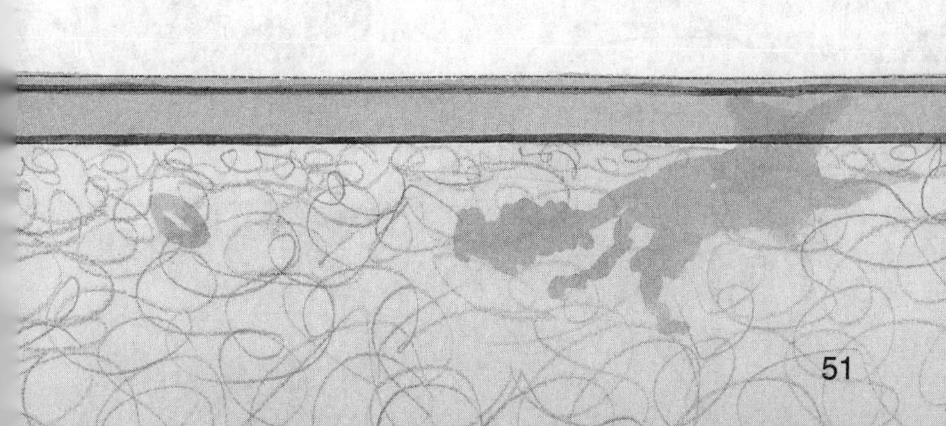

SHE'S RUNNING INTO THE LIVING ROOM!

GET HER!

SHE'S RUNNING UPSTAIRS!

GET HER!

SHE'S IN THE HALLWAY!

GET HER!

SHE'S IN THE BATHROOM! She's trapped. Now, all we have to do is calmly close the door, and we can begin her bath.

Uh-oh.

• CHAPTER THREE •

HOW TO GIVE KITTY A BATH

Now that you have Kitty, and the bath is prepared, please follow these simple steps carefully so that both you and she are comfortable during the bath.

1) Gently but firmly gather Kitty up in your arms.

2) Pet her and caress her lovingly to reassure Kitty that all is well.

3) Tell Kitty that you love her. No doubt, Kitty will tell you that she loves you, too.

4) Now, gently lower Kitty into the warm, soapy water for her bath.

I HAVE WRONGED YOU! AND TO MAKE UP FOR MY WRETCHED BEHAVIOR, I SHALL REWARD YOU . . .

FOR I AM NO
MERE KITTY!

I AM QUEEN ESMERELDA,*
KITTY OF MAGIC CANDY
RAINBOW ISLAND!

I HAVE BEEN SENT TO
YOUR LAND TO FIND THE
ONE WITH THE TRUEST
AND BRAVEST HEART, FOR
ONLY THE ONE WITH THE
TRUEST AND BRAVEST
HEART WOULD DARE TO
GIVE A DIRTY, SMELLY
KITTY A BATH!

AS A REWARD FOR YOUR
TRUE AND BRAVE HEART,
I BESTOW UPON YOU
THE GREATEST TREASURE
EVER GRANTED . . .

THIS FLYING GOLDEN UNICORN STANDING IN A MAGIC CAULDRON FILLED WITH CHOCOLATE-COVERED DIAMONDS!

We regret to
inform you that
Chapter Three
was a dream.

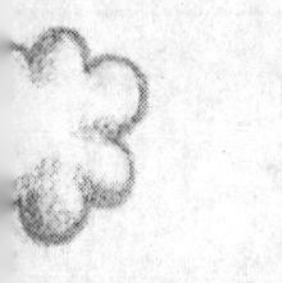

• CHAPTER FOUR •

GETTING KITTY INTO THE WATER

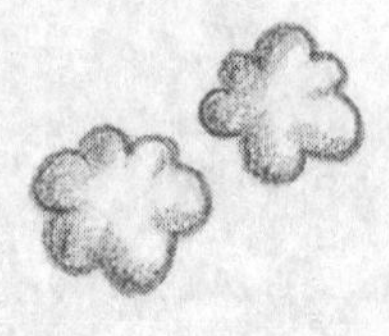

You must have known it would be harder than that.

Now that you've regained consciousness, you probably remember what happened when . . .

You took her to the vet.

You made her brush her teeth.

You made her take her medicine.
You clipped her nails.
You made her finish her vegetables.
Nick,
I'm sorry, but this image is much too gruesome and violent for us to publish in this book. If we were to show what Kitty did here, we would give the readers nightmares for at least fifty years.
Your editor,*
Neal

Well, none of that matters now, because Kitty . . . YOU STINK! And you NEED TO TAKE A BATH.

Tell Kitty in a firm voice that she needs to get into that bathtub NOW!

Okay. That didn't work.

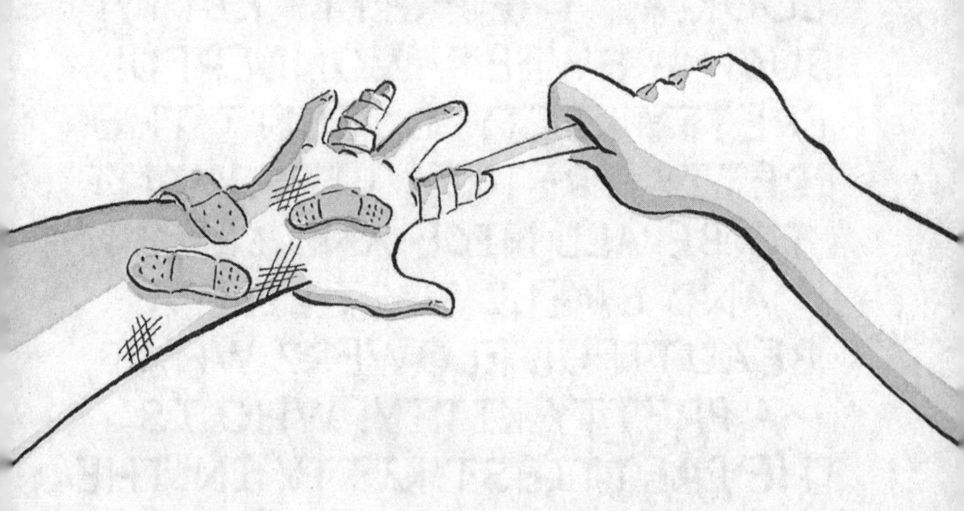

You might want to try the subtle art of NEGOTIATION.*

Negotiation is how you can use words instead of force to try and convince Kitty to do something she doesn't want to do.

First, try FLATTERY.

LOOK AT THE PRETTY KITTY!
SUCH A SWEET, WONDERFUL,
PRETTY KITTY! DOESN'T THE
PRETTY, PRETTY KITTY WANT
TO BE ALL NICE AND CLEAN
AND SMELL JUST LIKE A
BEAUTIFUL FLOWER? WHAT
A PRETTY KITTY! WHO IS
THE PRETTIEST KITTY IN THE
WHOLE WIDE WORLD?
YOU ARE! YES, YOU ARE!
YOU PRETTY, PRETTY,
SWEET LITTLE KITTY, YOU!

If that doesn't work, try . . .

. . . BEGGING.

PLEASE! PLEEEEASE!
PLEASE GET IN THE BATHTUB!
PLEEEASE!
IF THERE IS EVEN AN OUNCE
OF GOODNESS IN YOU,
WON'T YOU PLEEEASE
GET IN THE BATHTUB?
PLEEEASE!
I'VE WORKED SO HARD TO GET
YOU HERE AND NOW YOU'RE
ALMOST IN THE TUB! YOU'RE
SO CLOSE! WON'T YOU
PLEEEASE GET IN THE TUB?
PLEEEEEEEEEASE!

I'LL BE YOUR BEST FRIEND.

If that doesn't work, try . . .

. . . BRIBERY.

OH, KITTY . . . YOU KNOW THAT FANCY SCRATCHING POST MADE OUT OF SILK AND RHINOCEROS HIDE YOU LIKE? WELL, I'LL BUY IT FOR YOU IF YOU GET IN THE TUB. AND YOU LIKE THOSE GOAT TAIL AND SALMON FIN TREATS, DON'T YOU? I'LL BUY YOU THE BIGGEST BOX IN THE STORE IF YOU GET IN THE TUB. DID I SAY "BOX"? I MEANT "BARREL"! DID I SAY "BARREL"? I MEANT "TRUCKLOAD"! AND YOU CAN EAT THEM WHILE YOU TAKE YOUR BATH. DO WE HAVE A DEAL, KITTY?

KITTY?

If that doesn't work, try . . .

. . . REVERSE PSYCHOLOGY.*

OKAY . . . IF YOU DON'T WANT TO TAKE A BATH . . . FINE! DON'T TAKE A BATH. SEE IF I CARE. YOU'LL SMELL TERRIBLE FOR THE REST OF YOUR LIFE AND NO ONE WILL LIKE BEING NEAR YOU, BUT THAT'S OKAY BY ME. WHATEVER YOU DO, DON'T GET INTO THAT BATHTUB. THAT'S THE ONLY WAY YOU'LL GET CLEAN, AND WE WOULDN'T WANT THAT. I'M HAPPY YOU'RE NOT GOING TO TAKE A BATH. I REALLY AM. I HOPE YOU NEVER, EVER TAKE A BATH . . . UNLESS . . .

YOU REALLY WANT TO.

DO YOU?

Oh, well . . . It looks like Kitty is not going to be taking a bath after all. Sorry. We really tried, though.

Maybe we should just end the book right now and save some paper.

It really is too bad, because the only way we'll be able to give *Puppy* a bath is if Kitty goes first.

Didn't you know that, Kitty? Puppy is even dirtier and smellier than you. He's going to need an EXTRA SPECIAL BATH . . .

. . . with lots of
cold water . . .
EEK!

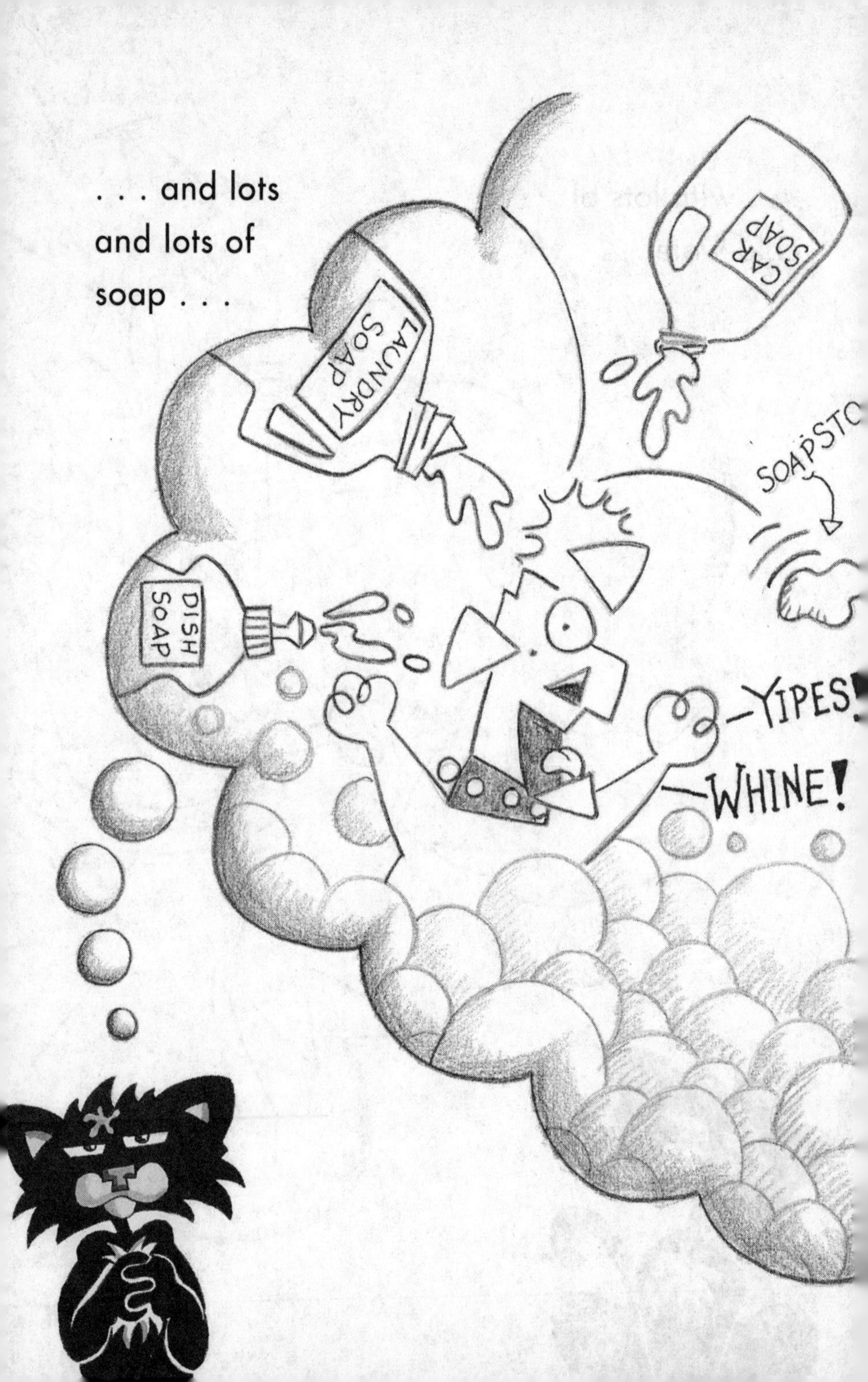
. . . and lots
and lots of
soap . . .
LAUNDRY SoAP
CAR SOAP
DISH SoAP
SOAPSTO
YIPES!
WHINE!

. . . and lots
and lots of
scrubbing!
TOILET BRUSH
PAINTBRUSH
TOOTHBRUSH
CHIMNEY BRUSH
AIEEE!
MERCY!
SNICKER

But, of course, that's never going to happen if Kitty doesn't take her bath first.

Well, I'll be . . .

• CHAPTER FIVE •

THE BATH

Now that you finally have Kitty in the bathtub, gently use a cup or small pot to pour warm bathwater over her to soak her fur.

Try not to pour water directly onto Kitty's head. Instead, use a soft, moist towel and gently wipe her face and head.

Use a cat shampoo recommended by Kitty's veterinarian to clean her dirty fur.

Rinse Kitty off using a handheld shower attachment if you have one. If not, gently pour water over her as you did earlier.

Again, try not to soak Kitty's head, and use that washcloth to wipe excess soap and water from her face.

Keep rinsing and soaking and wiping Kitty until you're absolutely certain you've removed all of the shampoo.

You may have noticed that Kitty's been making a lot of noise. She's probably trying to tell you something. The following is a list of common cat sounds and their meanings.

MEOW ⟶ I am hungry.

MEEE
OOO ⟶ I am very hungry.
WWW?

MEE
OOW
RRR ⟶ I'm pretty darn hungry, and you better feed me right now or suffer the horrible consequences.
OWW
RRR!

FFT! → I want to be alone.

HISSS! → Back off, pal!

MEOWR
REOWR → Unless you're really tired of living, please respect that I am in a very bad mood.
FFT!

MEOWR
REOWR
YEOWR
HISS
FFT
FFT
FFT
MEOWR!

→

Nick,

Sorry, but once again we can't print this. What Kitty says is so horrible and repulsive that we could all go to jail for the rest of our lives if this was printed.

Hope you understand.

Your editor,

Neal

You now have a very, very clean Kitty, even though she is also a very, very wet Kitty.

Gently remove her from the bathtub and drain the bathwater.

Dry Kitty off by wrapping her in a clean towel and rubbing her all over.

And Kitty will be nice and dry!

What a clean, sweet-smelling Kitty!

UNCLE MURRAY'S FUN FACTS

I'LL BE RIGHT BACK. I'M MAKING A SANDWICH!

CAN CATS SWIM?

Even though cats hate baths and aren't very big fans of water in general, ALL cats CAN swim. In fact, they're very good swimmers.

One breed of cat known as the Turkish Van loves to swim so much that they will jump in water whenever possible.

Tigers are also excellent swimmers. They live in very warm climates, so they tend to swim a lot to keep themselves cool.

If you're ever being chased by a tiger, don't bother jumping in the water. It won't help. Instead, climb a tree. Tigers love to swim, but they're not very good tree climbers.

And if you're ever around the wetlands of Nepal and Myanmar, look for the Fishing Cat. It's a breed of cat with long claws that never fully retract that dives into water to catch fish.

• CHAPTER SIX •

AFTER THE BATH

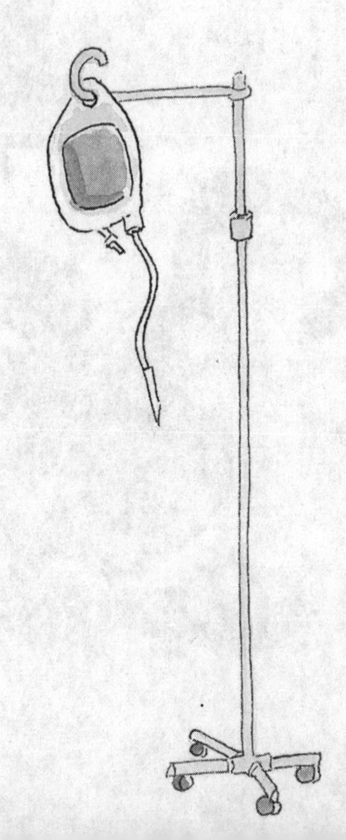

After the bath is done, Kitty will probably start licking herself quite a bit again. She'll want to be clean in the way she likes to be clean—cat-tongue clean.

This would *NOT* be a good time to pet her.

In fact, Kitty may avoid you altogether for a few hours . . . or days . . . or weeks.

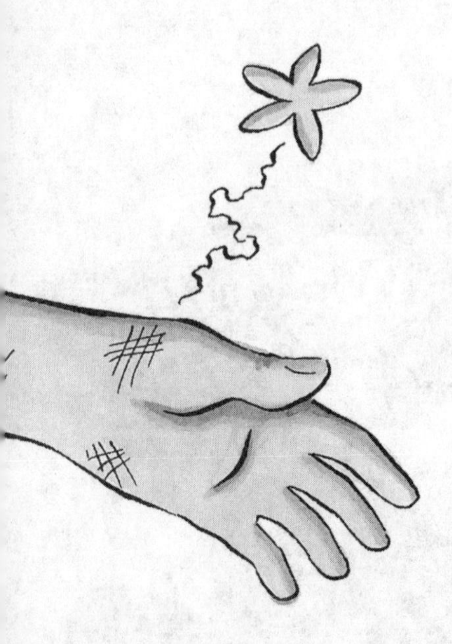

Try not to take it personally. After all, you made Kitty do something that she *HATED* and never wanted to do.

You still did the right thing. Kitty probably won't thank you now. She probably won't thank you EVER. She may even do little things in the next few days to tell you how angry she feels.

But if you had not given Kitty that bath, she would have licked herself while she was so very, very dirty. She could have become very, very sick. And neither you nor Kitty wants that!

You and Kitty may not always get along. But there are TWO things you both have in common.

1) You both know that someday Kitty will forgive you.

2) You both hope you NEVER have to give Kitty a bath again.

• EPILOGUE •

HOW TO GIVE PUPPY A BATH

STEP ONE:

STEP TWO:

STEP THREE:
TOWEL

• THE END •

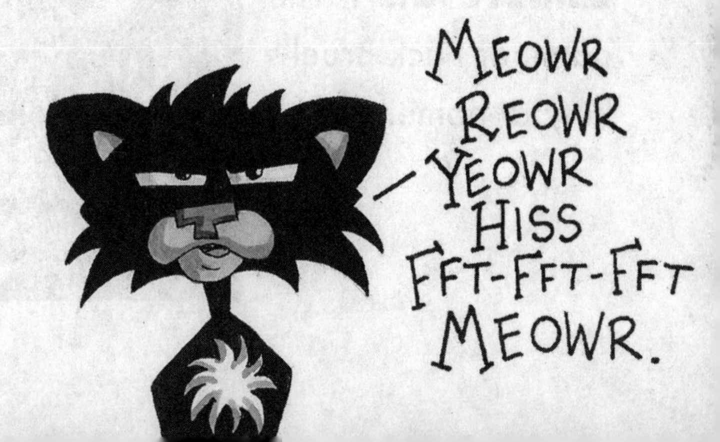
MEOWR
REOWR
YEOWR
HISS
FFT-FFT-FFT
MEOWR.

• GLOSSARY •

Bath • A word you should never say out loud around Kitty.

Combs and Wattles • Fleshy lobes often found on the heads and necks of chickens but rarely found on cats.

Editor • Someone who *brilliantly* supervises the publication of a book like this one *and really deserves most of the credit.*

Esmerelda • The name of Nick Bruel's kitty at home.

Glossary • A list of words and their definitions often found at the back of a book. You have five seconds to find the Glossary for THIS book. Go!

Negotiation • A process that works very well when trying to convince your parents to give you a bigger allowance, but very poorly when trying to convince Kitty she needs a bath.

Papillae • The hundreds of tiny little hooks on Kitty's tongue that make it feel like sandpaper when she licks your finger.

Plasma • The liquid part of blood. Blood cells float around in it to carry fuel and oxygen around the body. Without plasma, they would be like fish trying to swim without a river. Having some extra plasma around when giving Kitty a bath is useful in case you "lose" a little.

Reverse Psychology • A method you can use to get someone to do something by pretending that you want the opposite. But it never works, so don't try it.

Sofa • A soft, comfortable, and very expensive scratching post used by Kitty.

Vegetables • Another word you should probably never say out loud around Kitty.

Vet • An abbreviation of *veterinarian*. A veterinarian is a doctor for animals like Kitty and may be the bravest person on the planet.

BAD KITTY

Happy Birthday, BAD KITTY

NICK BRUEL

A NEAL PORTER BOOK
ROARING BROOK PRESS
New York

• CONTENTS •

•CHAPTER ONE•

GOOD MORNING, KITTY!

GOOD MORNING, KITTY!

Today is going to be a great day! The sun is shining! The birds are singing! Flowers are blooming everywhere with all the colors of the rainbow!

You know what today is, don't you, Kitty? Today is a very special day! Today is the kind of day that only comes once a year! Today is the kind of day that you celebrate ALL day long! Today is the kind of day that deserves a BIG, FUN PARTY!

Now, do you know what today is?

TODAY IS YOUR BIRTHDAY!!!

And that means we start your very special day with a very special **BIRTHDAY BREAKFAST!**

We made all of your favorites . . .

Aardvark Bagels, Clam Doughnuts, Eel Fritters, Grilled Hummingbirds, Iguana Jelly, Koala Lemonade, Mongoose and Nuts, Orangutan Pancakes, Quetzal Raisin bread, Snake Tortillas, Unicorn and Vegetable juice, Walrus in XO sauce, and for dessert a Yak Zabaglione!

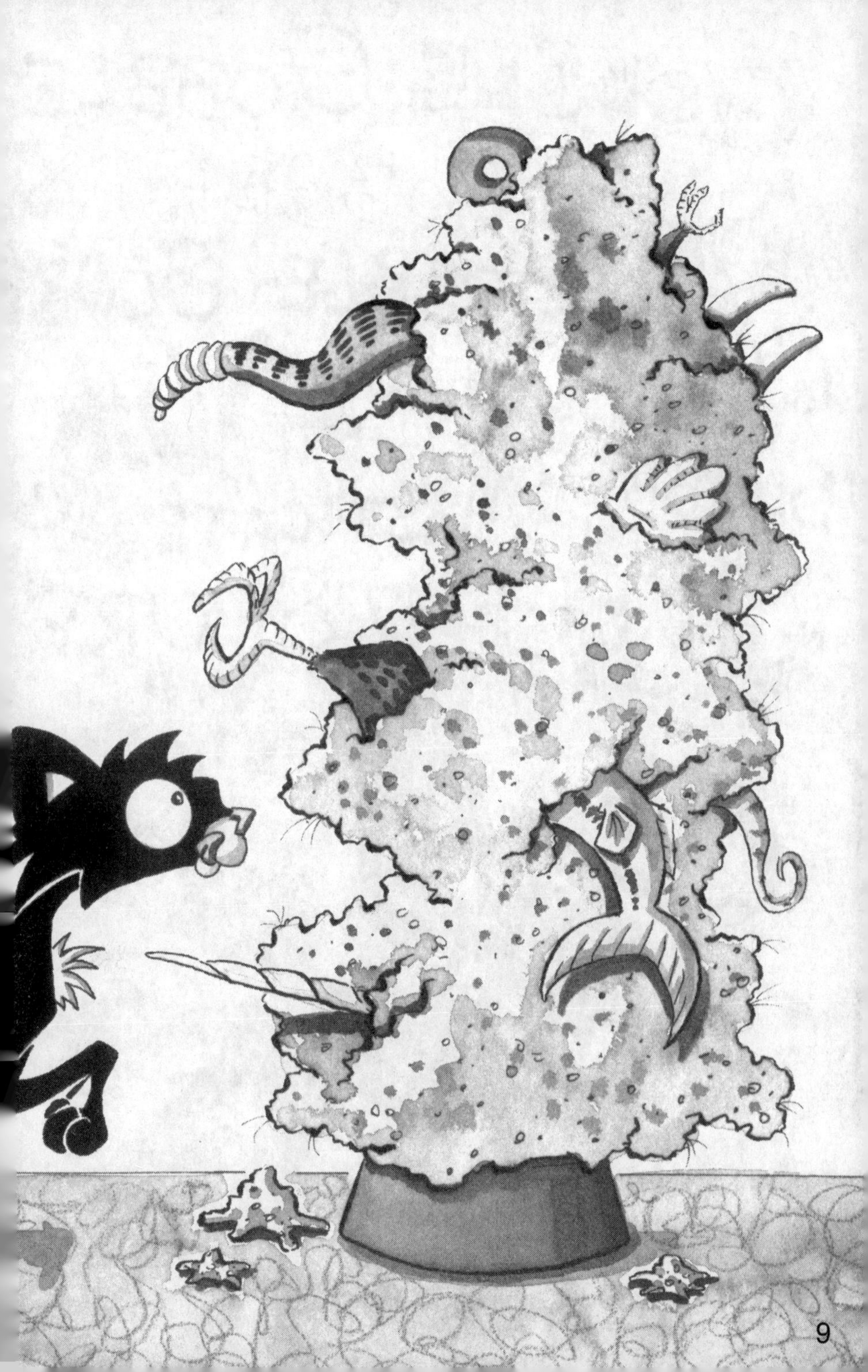

GOBBLE GOBBLE

SLOBBER

MUNCH GOBBLE SLURP

CHEW CHEW YUM

SLOBBER MASTICATE

GULP! SLURP

ZOOM

BURP
SNORE

Oh, come on, Kitty! You're not going to sleep all day again, are you? All you did yesterday was sleep. All you did the day before yesterday was sleep. And all you did the day before the day before yesterday was sleep.

Are you going to do nothing but sleep every single day?

The typical house cat will sleep an average of sixteen hours a day. That's more than TWICE what the average human being sleeps.

One reason cats sleep so much is because they're CREPUSCULAR, which means that they are most active at dawn and at dusk, when the sun is rising and when the sun is setting. Those are the times cats are used to hunting for their food.

Cats are also very light sleepers. Even when they might look like they're sound asleep, all of their senses are still very active. For instance, you can see their ears wiggle and turn while they're sleeping. This way, cats can remain aware of their surroundings even while they sleep and can wake up very quickly if they need to.

WHUMP!
AIEEEE!

Some big cats, like lions, will eat so much after a successful hunt that they will sleep for two straight days afterward. Often it is only the female lions that do the hunting while the male lions do most of the sleeping.

HEY! I LIKE THAT IDEA!
YO, JEANNIE!
GO GET ME A SANDWICH
AT THE DELI WHILE
I TAKE A NAP!

Okay, Kitty. I get it. You're just going to sleep all day again. I guess I'll just decorate the house all by myself. I guess I'll just blow up the balloons all by myself. I guess I'll just let all the guests in all by myself.

I guess I'll just **EAT THE CAKE** and **OPEN THE PRESENTS** all by myself.

Wow. Cats really can wake up quickly.

•CHAPTER TWO•

KITTY'S FIRST YEAR

Before we do anything else, Kitty, it's time for our favorite birthday tradition. It's time to look through the old photo album and remember all of those wonderful days from long ago.

LOOK, KITTY! Here's a picture of you back in the animal shelter where we found you.

Awww! You were SOOOOOOooooo cute!

You were the sweetest, kindest, nicest kitten in the whole shelter. And you were helpful, too!

You used to help keep all of the cages clean. You liked to read to all the other kittens. And you ALWAYS shared your food.

LOOK, KITTY! Here are pictures of your mother!

You and Mama Kitty were very close.

The day eventually came when it was time for you to leave the shelter. That's when you came home to live with us.

But you didn't want to go. You didn't want to leave Mama Kitty, even though you were old enough.

AW, HECK, JEANNIE! I WAS ONLY KIDDING ABOUT THE SANDWICH

UNCLE MURRAY'S FUN FACTS

WHEN ARE KITTENS OLD ENOUGH TO LEAVE THEIR MOTHERS?

Cats mature much faster than human beings. The typical house cat reaches adulthood when it is only twelve to eighteen months old. Human beings can barely walk at that age!

So when a cat is only twelve weeks old, it is probably old enough to leave its mother and go to a new home. Twelve weeks might seem very young to you and me, but to a cat it is perfectly normal.

It is very important not to remove a kitten from its mother before it is twelve weeks old.

Kittens learn a lot of important things from their mothers before they're adopted.

They learn how to use the litter box properly.

They learn how to eat solid food.

If you remove a kitten from its mother too early, the kitten might have a more difficult time learning these important lessons from you.

KITTENS . . . TWELVE WEEKS . . . LITTER BOX . . . GOT IT!
LOOK, I GOTTA RUN OUT AND BUY SOME FLOWERS!

We loved you right away, even though you were sometimes pretty . . . uh . . . grumpy.

Away from your mother, you weren't the same helpful little kitten that we first met. But we still love you.

Although, you don't always make it easy.

•CHAPTER THREE•

EVERY PARTY NEEDS DECORATIONS

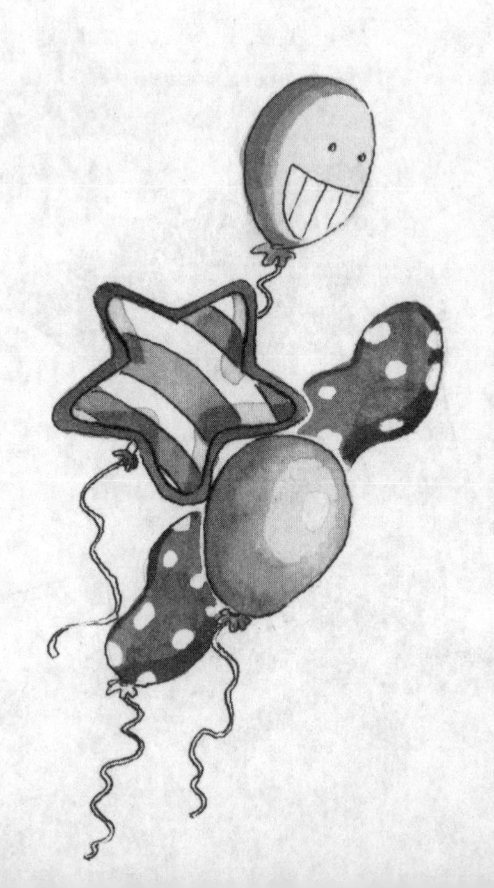

Okay, Kitty . . . Let's get started.

The first thing we do is pull out the box of decorations we use every year.

Why don't you help me blow up some balloons.

That's not helping, Kitty.

Okay. Why don't you help me hang some streamers.

That's not helping, Kitty.

Okay, Kitty . . . Why don't you help me put this incredibly delicate and valuable glass birthday vase that's been in my family for a dozen generations onto the mantel.

On second thought, maybe I'll just leave this in the box.

All right, Kitty . . . Since you don't want to help me blow up balloons or hang streamers, will you at least help me to set up the table for all the **PRESENTS** you're going to get?

That's right, Kitty. All I need you to do is help me spread the special birthday party tablecloth onto the table.

Thank you, Kitty. Now you're being helpful.

Gosh! The table looks so festive. Except . . . I think it's missing one little thing, Kitty. What do you think that one little thing is, Kitty?

It's missing **PRESENTS**, of course!

So, I'm going to put one there right now. It's a BIG surprise, Kitty. And I know it's something you REALLY want, Kitty . . . that you really, REALLY, **REALLY** want.

But you have to promise me that you won't open it until the party.

Remember, Kitty . . . You promised not to open the present yet. YOU PROMISED.

MILK
WHINE!
PUPPY
CAGE

Where are you going, Kitty? The guests will be here any minute now!

DIG-DIG
RUSTLE

THE GIANT
CAT-ALOG OF
CAT TOYS
I WANT
EVERYTHING!

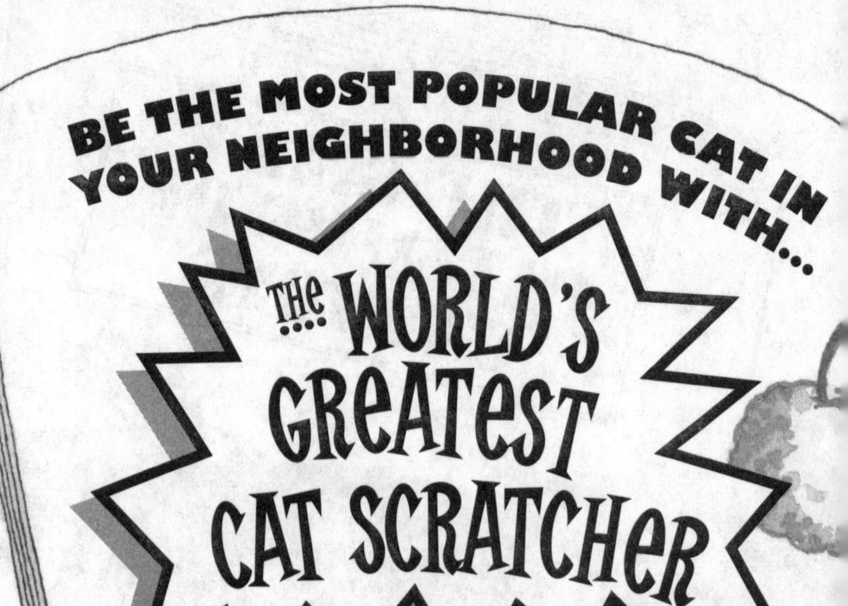

BE THE MOST POPULAR CAT IN YOUR NEIGHBORHOOD WITH...
THE WORLD'S GREATEST CAT SCRATCHER

Silk cushion stuffed with hummingbird feathers!

Baobab wood base lined with diamonds!

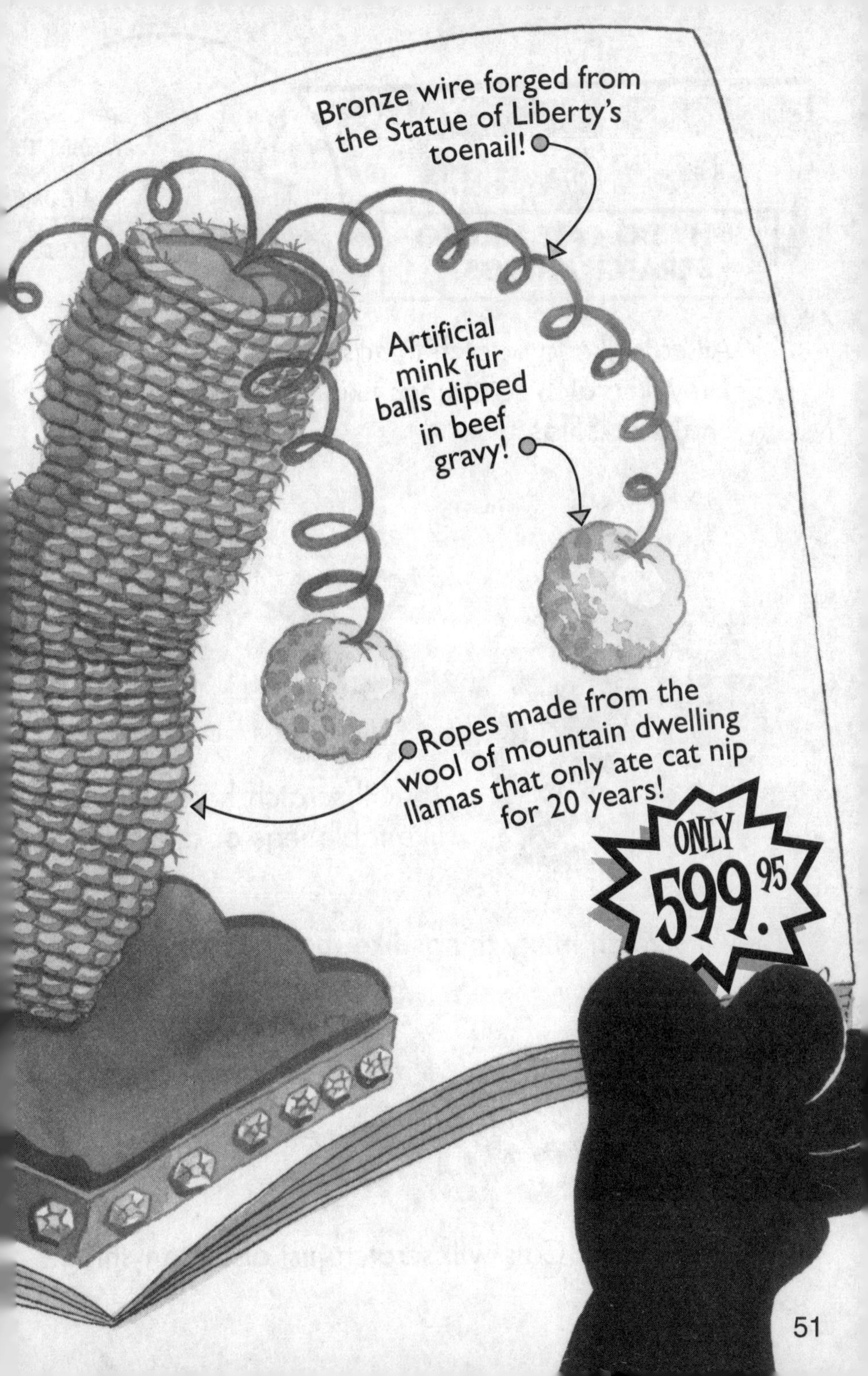
Bronze wire forged from the Statue of Liberty's toenail!
Artificial mink fur balls dipped in beef gravy!
Ropes made from the wool of mountain dwelling llamas that only ate cat nip for 20 years!
ONLY
599.95

UNCLE MURRAY'S FUN FACTS

WHY DO CATS LIKE TO SCRATCH THINGS?

HEY, JEANNIE! I BRUNG YA SOME PRETTY DAISIES!

All cats like to scratch things. They'll scratch soft things like chairs or sofas.

They'll scratch hard things like table legs or dressers.

They'll scratch fuzzy things like rugs or carpets.

Cats will scratch just about anything.

Sometimes they'll do it for fun or exercise. But they'll also scratch things because their claws are like our fingernails—they never stop growing. But unlike our fingernails, a cat's claws grows in layers. So cats will sometimes scratch something to rub off an old layer for a newer, fresher, sharper claw layer.

The scratch marks they leave behind are also very important for cats—they mark a cat's territory. Those scratches are territory markers for other cats to both see AND smell. Inside a cat's paw pads are little scent glands that leave little odors on anything they scratch. They act like messages for other cats to read.

GRAB!

DING-DONG!

The guests are here, Kitty! Let's meet them at the door.

•CHAPTER FOUR•

EVERY PARTY NEEDS GUESTS

IT'S BIG KITTY!

Big Kitty is the biggest kitty in the whole neighborhood!

Big Kitty is MUCH bigger than Kitty.

Big Kitty weighs MUCH more than Kitty.

EVERYTHING about Big Kitty is bigger. Even his hair balls are pretty darn big.

I sure hope we have enough birthday cake!

Even Big Kitty's present is BIG! Wow! I wonder what it could be!

Kitty, why don't you open your presents later when . . . Never mind.

Look, Kitty! It's a . . . dead mouse.

I guess it wasn't dead after all.

IT'S THE TWIN KITTIES!

The Twin Kitties are brother and sister and the cutest kitties in the whole neighborhood.

More than anything, they love to PLAY. And they love to play with Kitty!

On those rare occasions when Kitty is not in the mood to play with them . . .

. . . they play with Puppy!

Look, Kitty! They brought you not ONE but TWO presents! I wonder what's in them.

Look, Kitty! It's a ball of string and a ball of twine. How thoughtful.

I'll just put them on the present table where they'll be safe.

IT'S STINKY KITTY!

Stinky Kitty is the—***cough***—stinkiest kitty in the whole—***choke***—neighborhood.

He never brushes his teeth.

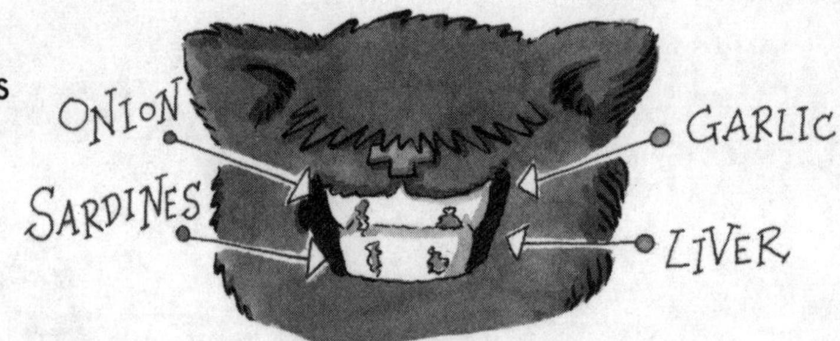

He's always getting dirty.

He likes to sleep in his litter box.

But Stinky Kitty did—***cough***—bring you a very nice-looking present. I wonder what it—***hack***—is!

Look, Kitty! It's an . . . old cardboard paper towel tube.

Oh well, Kitty. It's the thought that counts. Let's put it on the presents table where it will be safe.

IT'S CHATTY KITTY!

MEOW
MEOW
MEOW
MEOW
MEOW
MEOW
MEOWMEOW
MEOW-MEOW
MEOW
MEOW
MEOW
MEOW
MEOW
MEOW
MEOW
MEOW
MEOW
MEOW
MEOW
MEOW*
SHHH

*A funny thing happened to me on the way to the party. I saw a stick that was shaped just like a chicken bone only it didn't smell like a chicken bone at all. Mostly, it smelled like a stick. I find that sticks almost never smell like chicken bones unless you were to rub the stick with a chicken bone, but why would you do that?

Chatty Kitty is the . . .

She likes to . . .

And she likes to . . .

And she even likes to . . .

Never mind.

* Why do you suppose oranges are called "oranges?" Do you think it's because they are colored orange, or is the color orange called "orange" because it's the color of oranges? I wonder why all fruits aren't named after their colors. Grapes could be called "purples" and a bunch of grapes could be called a "bunch of purples," unless they're white grapes, which really aren't white at all but more of a pale green. But you'd still have to be careful because if you asked for a "bunch of purples," someone might give you a big pile of eggplants, which would just be silly, because cats don't eat eggplants. Or grapes. Or oranges either.

Chatty Kitty has brought you such a nice-looking present. Why don't you open it right now! (Do you think I could borrow some of that paper to put in my ears?)

MEOW
MEOW
MEOW
MEOW
MEOW
MEOW
MEOW
MEOW
MEOW
MEOW
MEOW
MEOW
MEOW
MEOW
MEOW
MEOW
MEOW
MEOW
MEOW
MEOW
*

*A moth got into the house the other day, only I wasn't sure if it was a moth or a butterfly because it was big like a butterfly but brown and gray like a moth, and I tried to catch it but it flew too high for me, which is good because some butterflies are poisonous if you eat them, which is gross, but sometimes I can't help myself. It didn't matter, though, because it turned out to be just a feather anyway.

Look, Kitty! It's . . . a collection of old mothballs she found in the closet.

MEOW
MEOW
MEOW
MEOW *

*They also ward off butterflies. **Don't eat them!**

I guess kitties aren't the best gift givers. Oh, well. Let's put them on the table where they'll be safe.

DING-
DONG

IT'S PRETTY KITTY!

Pretty Kitty is the prettiest kitty in the whole neighborhood.

And she knows it.

She's won over a dozen cat shows.

All of the boy kitties are madly in love with her.

Even the present that Pretty Kitty brought is pretty. It's almost too pretty to . . .

Look, Kitty! It's some tufts of Pretty Kitty's pretty fur.

Oh, Kitty. Don't be like that. It's such pretty fur. That fur has won prizes at cat shows. I'll put it on the present table where it will be safe.

IT'S STRANGE KITTY!

Strange Kitty is the oddest kitty in the whole neighborhood . . . maybe even the whole world. In fact, some people aren't convinced he really is a kitty.

Unlike all of the other kitties, he has no fur.

Unlike all of the other kitties, he wears a hat and necktie.

Unlike all of the other kitties, he would rather sit and read comic books by himself than scratch things or chase mice or sleep all day.

Look, Kitty!
I think Strange
Kitty brought
you a
present, too!

He brought
you a comic
book! Isn't that
nice? Say
"Thank you!"

That's not how we say
"Thank you," Kitty.
It's a very thoughtful
gift. I'll put it on the
present table where
it will be safe.

HEY! Where are all of the other presents I put there?

Where is the comic book Strange Kitty just gave you?

Kitty, did YOU do something with all of the presents?

No?

Well, if you didn't do something with all of your presents, then . . .

•CHAPTER FIVE•

WHO STOLE KITTY'S PRESENTS?

Kitty is certain that another kitty must have stolen all of her presents. After all, who but another kitty would even WANT a cardboard paper towel tube, a ball of string, a ball of twine, a collection of old mothballs, some tufts of cat fur, and an old comic book?

But Kitty thinks there is only one kitty—ONE kitty who could be capable of such a diabolical plot—only ONE kitty could pull off such a hideous crime—only ONE kitty who would rejoice in ruining a perfectly good birthday party by STEALING all of the birthday presents. **AND THAT KITTY IS . . .**

BIG KITTY

HEIGHT: Very, very tall.

WEIGHT: Weighs about the same as a large cinder block.

LAST SEEN: Eating ten pounds of sausages.

Only Big Kitty is big and strong enough to carry all of those presents home!

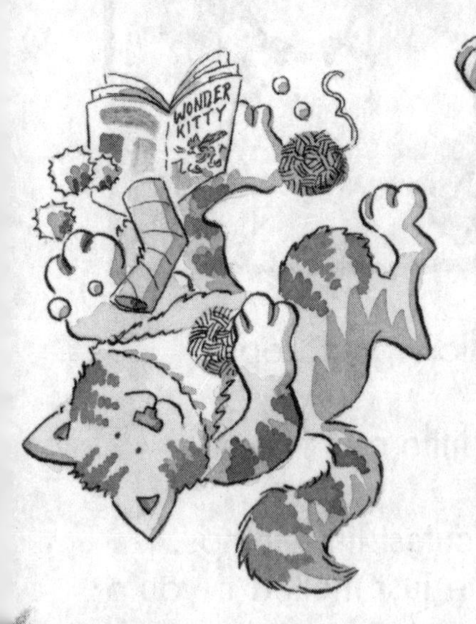

That's where he will play with them all by himself while laughing—LAUGHING—at Kitty.

But Big Kitty doesn't have the presents!
So the guilty kitty must be . . .

THE TWIN KITTIES

EYES: Like four cute little yellow gumdrops.

NOSES: Like a pair of cute little red buttons.

LAST SEEN: Doing just the cutest little things. I swear, your heart would have just melted if you'd seen it. They are just so darling!

It would have been easy for one of them to stand guard while the other one stole all of the presents!

They will add the presents to their own massive collection of toys from which they will build a mountain so that they can look down at Kitty and laugh—LAUGH!

But the Twin Kitties don't have the presents!

So the guilty kitty must be . . .

STINKY KITTY

EYES: No one—***cough***—dares get close enough to find out.

FUR: Dark gray. But might really be white.

LAST SEEN: Rummaging through the—***hack***—dumpster behind the fish market.

Stinky Kitty probably used his horrendous odor to distract everyone while he stole the presents!

Then he'll bury them in his litter box where no one would ever look and survive to tell the story. And then he will laugh—LAUGH!

But Stinky Kitty doesn't have the presents!

So the guilty kitty must be . . .

CHATTY KITTY

EYES: What?

FUR: Huh? What? Say that again.

FUR: How's that?

LAST SEEN: Sorry. I just can't hear you.

* Maybe all of your presents rolled under the sofa. That happens to me all the time. Once I found a crumpled-up piece of paper and was playing with it until it rolled under the sofa. I waited for a while, but it didn't come back out until one day someone moved the sofa to clean under it and there was the paper, so I played

She must have stolen the MEOW

MEOW MEOW MEOW MEOW MEOW MEOW

MEOW MEOW MEOW MEOW MEOW

And then she . . .

MEOW MEOW MEOW MEOW MEOW MEOW MEOW MEOW MEOW MEOW

And then she must have . . .

MEOW MEOW MEOW MEOW MEOW MEOW MEOW

EOW MEOW MEOW MEOW MEOW

EOW MEOW MEOW MEOW MEOW MEOW

EOW MEOW MEOW MEOW MEOW*

Never mind.

Chatty Kitty doesn't have the presents!

So the guilty kitty must be . . .

with it some more until it rolled under a set of drawers. I waited for a while, but it didn't come back out until one day someone moved them to clean in back, and there was the paper, so I played with it until it rolled under the sofa again. I waited for a while, but it didn't come back out until . . .

PRETTY KITTY

EYES: Like a pair of deep blue lakes at dawn's light.
FUR: Like a field of freshly fallen snow on a crisp winter's day.
LAST SEEN: Winning first prize at a DOG show—she is THAT pretty.

It must have been Pretty Kitty. Because she's jealous.

She was probably jealous because none of the presents were for her.

So she's going to make all of the boy kitties carry the presents back to her place. And then she will laugh—LAUGH—**LAUGH!**

But Pretty Kitty doesn't have the presents!
So the guilty kitty must be . . .

STRANGE KITTY

FUR: None.
HAT: Black.
LAST SEEN: At a comic-book convention debating about which underwater superhero was most powerful: Captain Poseidon or Mudskipper Lass.

Strange Kitty is a big weirdo. Not only is he the only kitty left, he's DIFFERENT. He must be the guilty kitty!

He probably took all of the presents and hid them under his hat. He probably has all of the stolen presents under his hat RIGHT NOW!

Strange Kitty is such an oddball. He's always pretending to be something he's not . . .

. . . like a superhero.

. . . or a swash-buckling pirate.

HE TOOK HIS VORPAL SWORD IN HAND...
GOTTA DANCE!

. . . or a brave dragon slayer.

. . . or a famous Broadway dancer.

He is such a strange kitty.

Well, if Strange Kitty didn't take the presents, then who did? This is quite a mystery.

Puppy? Is that a piece of string caught on your ear? Is that a tuft of Pretty Kitty's fur stuck on your forehead? Is that an old mothball sticking out from between your toes?

Uh-oh.

•CHAPTER SIX•

EVERY PARTY NEEDS A PIÑATA

RUN, PUPPY, RUN!

They think you stole Kitty's presents!

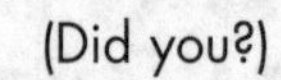

(Did you?)

MEOW
MEOW
MEOW

KITTIES! KITTIES! PLEASE!

I'm sure Puppy has a very good explanation.

(Don't you?)

BIG BOOK OF ROBOTS
MEOW
EOW
W
MIGHTY
OG

OH NO!

Puppy is all tangled up in electrical cords and speaker wires!

COOL!
MELVIN COMICS

EGADS!

What do you naughty kitties think you're doing with Puppy?

WHOA!
NICE!
SUPER-WORM

JUMPIN' JEHOSHAPHAT!

The kitties want to use Puppy as a piñata!

MEOW
MEOW
MEOW
DO YOU HAVE ANY "MEGA MOUSE?"
YUP.
THE RED BIRD

NO, KITTIES, NO!

Puppy does not have candy inside of him! I swear!

Something must be done or Puppy could get hurt. But what can we do?

WAIT! I know . . .

What three words can bring peace to all nations? What three words can create order out of chaos? What three words can soothe the savage instincts of a bunch of kitties that have lost all control?

MEOW
MEOW
WHEN DID
HE GET
FREEZE
VISION?
ISSUE
#152.
MEGA
MOUSE

WHO WANTS CAKE?!

•CHAPTER SEVEN•

EVERY PARTY NEEDS CAKE

That's right, Kitties. Because this is a very special birthday, we have a very special birthday cake. It's made out of all of your favorite foods!

THE TWIN KITTIES LOVE CHICKEN LEGS
CHATTY KITTY LOVES PORK CHOPS
PRETTY KITTY LOVES CAVIAR
MEOW!
MEOW!
WOW!

BIG KITTY
LOVES
SARDINES
STINKY
KITTY
LOVES
LIMBURGER
CHEESE
SUPERHERO
TRADING CARDS
FOR STRANGE
KITTY
WHO'S YOUR
FAVORITE
MEMBER?
THE
PHENOMENAL
TUSK!
MEGA-E

And the icing is made out of Kitty's very favorite food! Liver!

What's wrong, Kitty? Don't you like your cake?

Kitty, are you upset because it's not a CHOCOLATE cake? I know you wanted a chocolate cake, but I already explained to you why you can NEVER have a chocolate cake.

Sorry.

DO YOU THINK THE TUSK IS STRONGER THAN CONCRETE LASS?
YUP.

UNCLE MURRAY'S FUN FACTS

WHY IS CHOCOLATE BAD FOR CATS?

CHOCOLATE! GOOD IDEA!

If you offer a cat some chocolate, she'll probably eat it. If you offer a cat some chocolate cake, she'll probably eat it.

But chocolate is like POISON to cats! So never offer it to them!

Chocolate contains a chemical compound called THEOBROMINE that is harmless to human beings but very dangerous for cats.

If a cat eats chocolate, she can become very sick and, yes, maybe even die.

So it's very important that you never leave chocolate lying around that a cat might eat by accident.

And the same goes for dogs and most birds. It's very important to keep chocolate away from all of your pets at home.

BUT IT'S OKAY TO GIVE IT TO YOUR AUNT JEANNIE! SHE LOVES CHOCOLATE!

Uh-oh. Kitty is starting to lose her temper. We better do something FAST.

Kitty! Don't tell me you've forgotten about the **BIG PRESENT** I gave you this morning! Don't you want to open it now?!

I know this is something you've been wanting for a very long time! Well, your wait is finally over, because you now have your very own . . .

STRONGER THAN THE SLAB?
NOT THE SLAB.

BIG WINTER SWEATER!
And it looks just adorable on you.

HAVE YOU READ THE ONE WHERE THE SLAB EATS THE MOON?
NO WAY! COOL!

Oh no! The sweater didn't work! I don't understand why! And I think Kitty is about to lose it if we don't do something right away.

WAIT! I almost forgot!
Look, Kitty! I almost forgot to give you one last present. It's even better than a big winter sweater! It's . . .
I HAVE IT AT MY PLACE! DO YOU WANNA COME OVER AND READ IT TOGETHER?
I SURE DO!

A MATCHING HAT AND BOOTIES!

Don't you just love them, Kitty? And they fit you perfectly! The nice lady at the cat sweater store told me they don't make this pattern anymore. No other kitty in the whole world owns this sweater and this hat and these booties.

Aren't you
LUCKY?!

Now, wait here while I go get the camera. This will make a great Christmas card. Then everyone we know will see just how very, very cute you look!

Kitty?

Are you okay, Kitty?

Uh-oh.

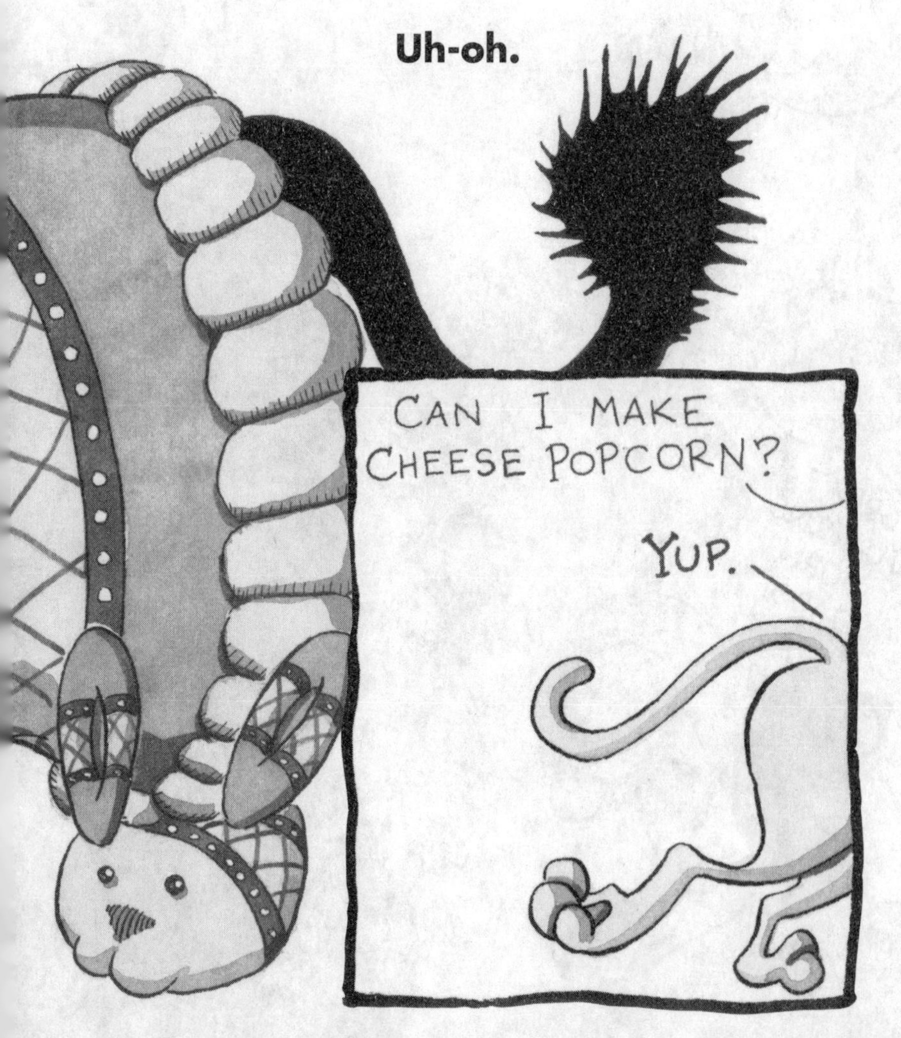

RUN FOR YOUR LIVES!
Kitty's having a major freak-out!
GREAT JUMPING HORN TOADS! *
* MEOW! MEOW! MEOW!

We woke her up when all
she wanted was to sleep!

She didn't get the gifts she wanted! And most of the gifts she did get are still missing!

She didn't like the balloons or the decorations!

She didn't get to hit the piñata!

She didn't even get the cake she wanted!

Head for the door, kitties! And don't stop until you're safe at home!

Thanks for coming, kitties. I hope you had a good time. See you next year!

•CHAPTER EIGHT•

THE PARTY'S OVER

Well, Kitty . . . I hope you're happy.

The decorations are ruined. The cake is ruined. Your new sweater is ruined. And all of your party guests have fled the house, running for their lives.

Just like last year. And the year before that. And the year before that. *Sigh*

You know what, Kitty? Sometimes . . . just sometimes . . . you are a truly **BAD KITTY**.

Oh, hush, Kitty. It's probably just one of the other kitties coming back because she forgot something.

Or maybe not.

Maybe it's a nice surprise for you.

Why don't you open the door to find out.

MEOW?

LICK

Well, Kitty. I guess you got what you wanted for your birthday after all.

•CHAPTER NINE•

GOOD NIGHT, KITTY

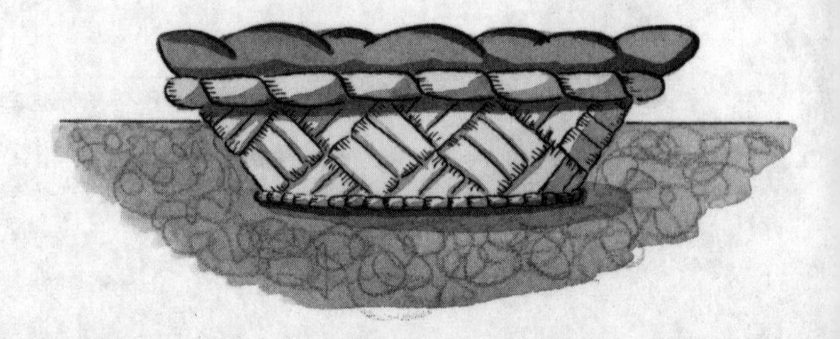

Good-bye, Mama Kitty. It was good seeing you again.

Maybe Kitty and I will go visit YOU someday.

What a fun day this has been, Kitty. Wasn't it great to see Mama Kitty again? Weren't all of those balloons and streamers just lovely before you destroyed, demolished, decimated, and shredded them all? Wasn't it great to see all of your friends again, even though you did chase them out of the house when you went berserk? Wasn't that a beautiful cake you sprayed on the walls?

Well, the day's not over yet, Kitty! There's one more surprise left for you on your birthday! Puppy worked very hard to make something extra special for you.

Look, Kitty! It's . . .

THE WORLD'S WORST CAT SCRATCHER!

CARDBOARD
PAPER TOWEL
TUBE

OLD
COMIC
BOOK

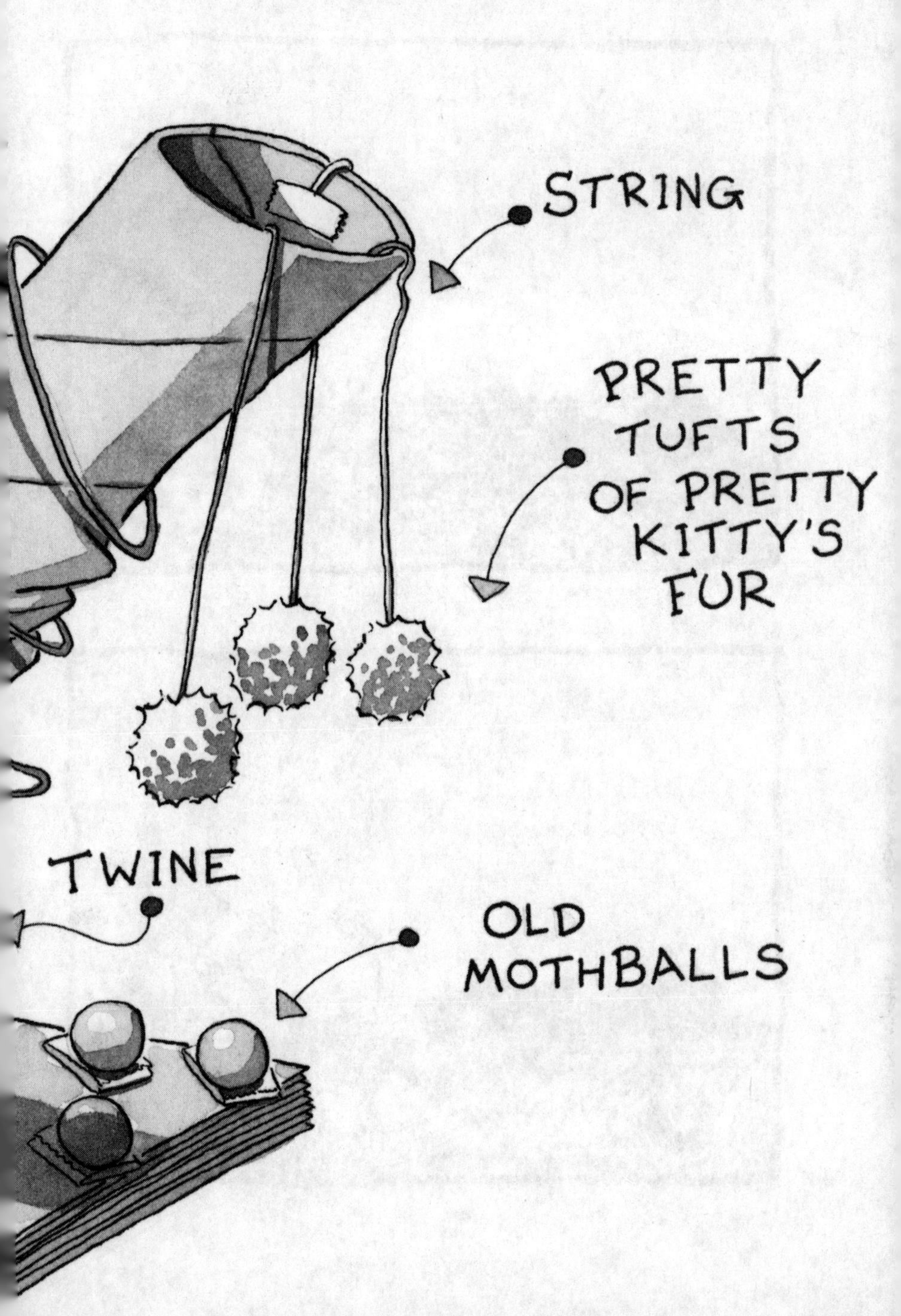
STRING
PRETTY TUFTS OF PRETTY KITTY'S FUR
TWINE
OLD MOTHBALLS

SCRATCH

TREMBLE

POOF!

SLURP!

Good night, Kitty.

• APPENDIX •

What Was That Kitty's Breed?

Even though all domestic cats, or house cats, are the same species, different characteristics like behavior and appearance separate one type of cat from another. Each of the kitties that came to the birthday party represented a different breed of cat.

Big Kitty is a Maine coon cat, one of the largest cat breeds. The males can weigh as much as eighteen pounds. They derived their name Coon cats because their long hair and bushy, striped tails make them resemble raccoons. Some people think the first Maine coon Cat came from a group of six pet cats sent to Maine by Marie Antoinette when she was planning to escape from France during the French Revolution.

The Twin Kitties are American shorthair cats. American shorthairs come in a variety of eighty different colors and patterns. Though they are called American shorthairs, the first ones came from Europe with early settlers. There are even records that show they were on the *Mayflower*.

Stinky Kitty is a Persian cat, the number one breed in popularity thanks to their easygoing personality. Although Persians aren't known to be any stinkier than other breeds of cats, they do require daily combings of their dense, long fur and even occasional baths. Because their legs are short, they don't jump very high. But they do like to run.

MEOW
MEOW
MEOW
MEOW
MEOW
MEOW
MEOW
MEOW

Chatty Kitty is a Siamese cat, a breed that originated in Thailand, but back in the 1800s Thailand was known as Siam. Siamese cats are considered one of the oldest breeds. Many other breeds such as the Burmese and the ocicat have been derived from the Siamese. And, yes, they are well known for being . . . talkative.

Pretty Kitty is a Turkish Angora cat, a breed that originated in the mountainous regions of Turkey where a long, thick coat of fur would be useful during their harsh winters. The Turkish Angora is considered such a national treasure that in 1917 the government of Turkey and the Ankara Zoo began a program that continues to this day to preserve the breed.

Strange Kitty is a sphynx cat, a natural mutation that was first seen in Toronto, Canada, in 1966. Most sphynx cats have absolutely no fur on their bodies except for a very fine fuzz, and they may not even have whiskers. This means that if they sit under the sun too long, they can actually get a sunburn. Because their skin is unprotected by fur, they need to take baths at least once a week.

In memory of Sam and Hercules,
Zou-zou, Halloween, Tom, Lucky, Choo-choo,
and all of my other pets I have loved and not forgotten.

An imprint of Macmillan Publishing Group, LLC
120 Broadway
New York, NY 10271
mackids.com

 Printed in the United States of America
by Lakeside Book Company, Harrisonburg, Virginia.

Cataloging-in-Publication Data is on file at the Library of Congress.

Originally published in the United States by Neal Porter Books,
an imprint of Roaring Brook Press
First Square Fish Edition: 2010
Square Fish logo designed by Filomena Tuosto

ISBN 978-0-312-62902-1 (Square Fish paperback)

ISBN 978-1-250-86481-9 (special edition)
1 3 5 7 9 10 8 6 4 2

AR: 3.6 / F&P: P / LEXILE: 610L

BAD KITTY VS the BABYSITTER

BAD KITTY VS the BABYSITTER

Previously titled
Bad Kitty vs Uncle Murray

NICK BRUEL

ROARING BROOK PRESS
New York

SQUARE FISH

An imprint of Macmillan Publishing Group, LLC

Printed in the United States of America by Lakeside Book Company, Harrisonburg, Virginia. For information, address Square Fish, 120 Broadway, New York, NY 10271.

Library of Congress Control Number: 2020909117

Originally published in the United States by Neal Porter Books,
an imprint of Roaring Brook Press
First Square Fish Edition: May 2011
Square Fish logo designed by Filomena Tuosto
mackids.com

ISBN 978-1-250-83584-0 (Square Fish paperback)

ISBN 978-1-250-86481-9 (special edition)
1 3 5 7 9 10 8 6 4 2

AR: 2.9 / LEXILE: 620L

To Neal

• CONTENTS •

•CHAPTER ONE•

PUSSYCAT PARADISE

WELCOME, KITTY!

Welcome to Pussycat Paradise, where everything you see is made entirely out of **FOOD**—food for your belly!

The mountains are made out of kibble. The trees are made out of sausages and bacon. Cans of cat food grow out of the ground. And the grass is made out of catnip.

Yes, Kitty! Eat! EAT! Food is everywhere! The rocks are made out of turkey and giblets. The dirt is made out of tuna fish. Even the rivers flow with beef gravy.

And the best part, of course, is that YOU are the only one here! No dogs to hound you. No people to make you take a bath. There is no one else here. Only you.

Be careful, Kitty. Don't touch that can. It's the only thing holding up that gigantic chicken liver.

OH NO! TOO LATE! The gigantic chicken liver is going to fall! Look out, Kitty! LOOK OUT!!

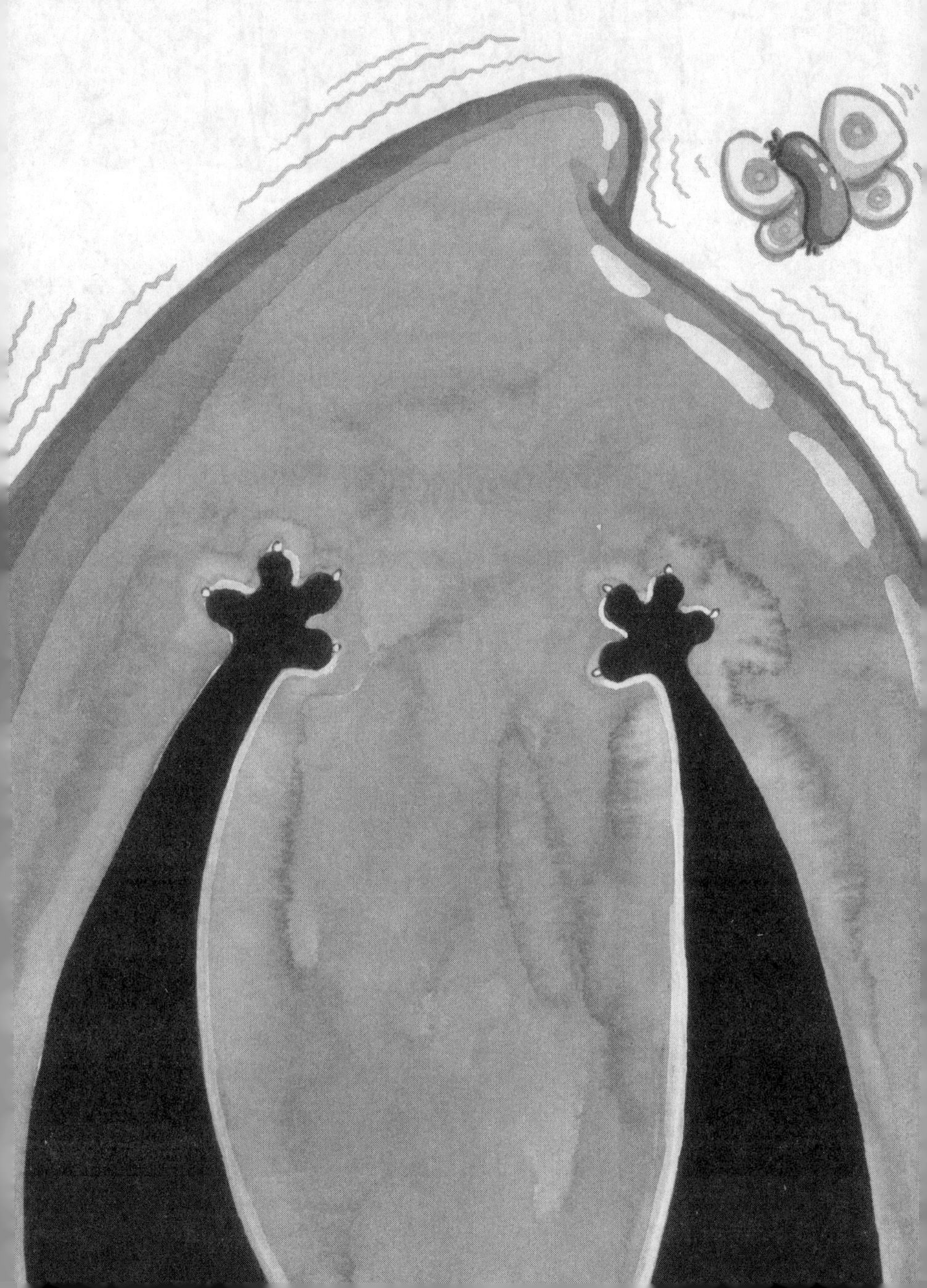

THUMP!

WHOOPS!

Sorry, Kitty. I hope I didn't wake you when I dropped the suitcase.

That's right, Kitty. We're going on a little trip. We'll be gone for a while.

Sorry, Kitty. You're not going with us. You'll have to stay home with Puppy.

Oh, don't be like that, Kitty. We'll be back in just a week. And when we get back, we'll have a REALLY BIG SURPRISE for you!

That's right, Kitty. **A REALLY BIG SURPRISE!** You like surprises, don't you?

In the meantime, Kitty, you won't be alone. We found someone who's going to stay here and feed you and take good care of you and Puppy while we're gone.

In fact, that must be him!

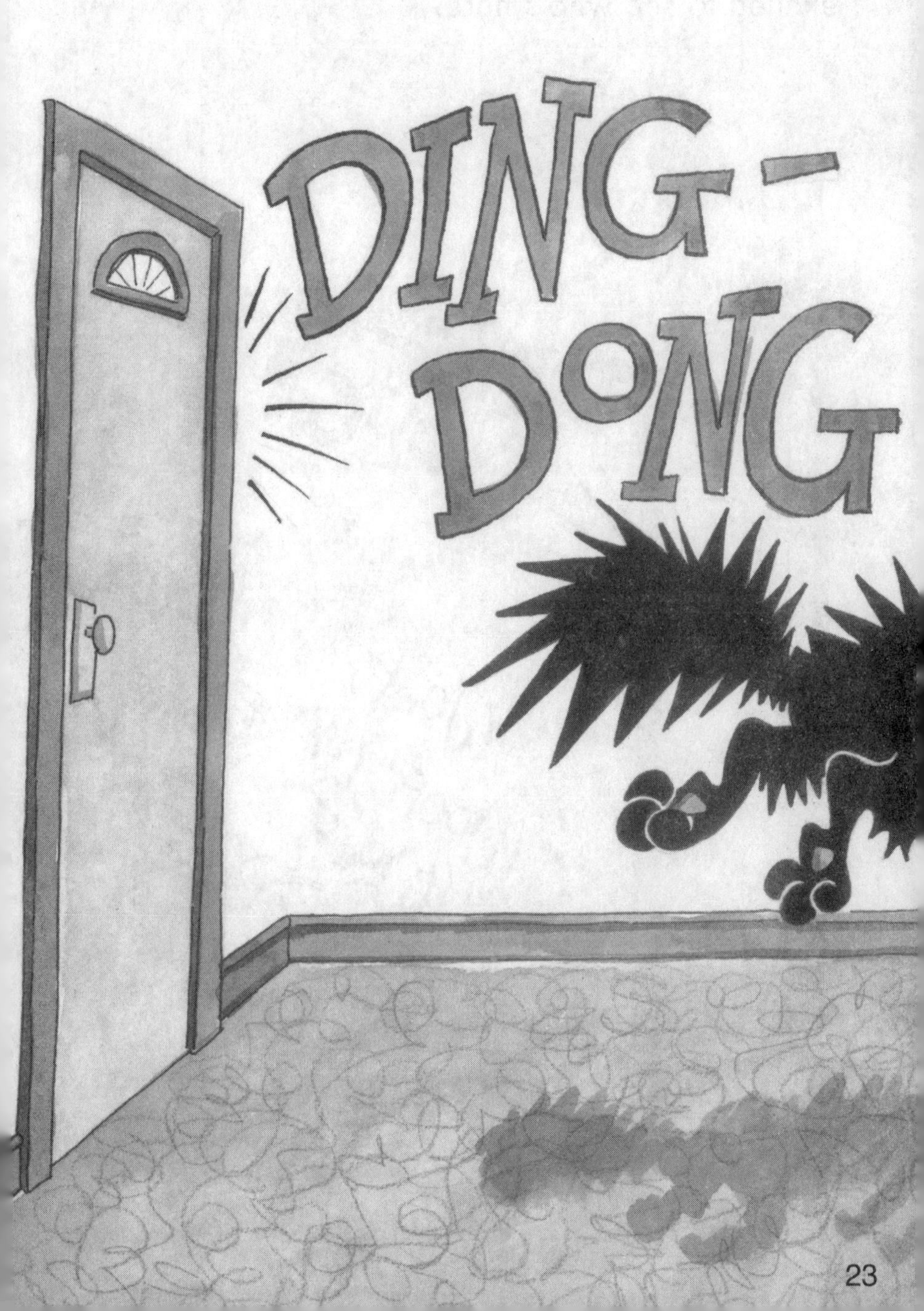

Where did Kitty go? Oh, well. At least Puppy is excited to see who's here.

IT'S GOOD OL' UNCLE MURRAY!

There you are, Kitty. Don't you want to say "Hi" to good ol' Uncle Murray?

Awww! You're a good dog, aren't you?

Hi there, ya
goofy cat!

GET IN MY MOUTH SO I CAN BITE YOU AND TASTE YOU AND CHEW YOU WITH MY BIG, SHARP TEETH!

Why are you looking at me like that,
ya goofy cat?

AND THEN I WILL
SWALLOW YOU AND
YOU WILL BE IN MY
BIG, FAT BELLY!
MWAH-HAH-HAH-HAH!

SCREEECH!

What the heck was THAT all about?

UNCLE MURRAY'S FUN FACTS

I was just wondering about that.

WHY ARE SOME CATS AFRAID OF PEOPLE?

No one ever talks about a "scaredy-giraffe" or a "scaredy-penguin" or even a "scaredy-dog," but everyone's heard of "scaredy-cats"! That's because cats use fear as a very valuable tool for survival.

The average weight for a cat is only around 10 pounds. Imagine what your life would be like if you lived with someone who was almost TWENTY TIMES BIGGER than you! That's what life is like for a cat living with a human being. Having good reflexes to avoid being stepped on or sat upon is very important.

CAT: AROUND 10 POUNDS.

BIG, FAT, GOOFY-LOOKING AUTHOR OF THIS BOOK: 185 POUNDS.

REALLY? DOES THIS BOOK MAKE ME LOOK FAT?

But sometimes a cat's fear of people can become exaggerated. Sometimes this happens when a kitten is raised without any human contact. It can also happen if a cat or a kitten has had a bad experience with a person.

But I'm a nice guy! I wouldn't hurt a fly, much less a dog or a cat, no matter how goofy it is.

It doesn't matter. A cat's instinct always tells her to be careful around people, especially strangers. The best way to get a cat to grow used to you is to be patient, be gentle, be quiet, and try not to take the cat's reaction to you too personally.

And one more thing . . . Try not to make any sudden, loud noises. Cats hate that.

No loud, sudden noises. Got it! What kind of jerk do you think I am? Everybody knows that!

Bye, Uncle Murray! Thank you for taking care of Kitty and Puppy while we're gone. We'll see you in a week!

By the way, you have to really push hard on this door to close it. If you don't, it won't really shut properly.
Okey doke! Goodbye! Good luck!

MEOW WOOF ARF
HISS
CRASH
KABLAM
BARK
FFT FFT
BOOM
HISS
MEOW

CREAK
Hoo-boy. Something tells me this is going to be a looooong week.

•CHAPTER TWO•

HIDE!

You know what, dog . . . I think the best thing to do right now is to sit down, relax, have some lunch, and maybe watch a little . . .

SCREEECH

Great. Now I gotta find something to clean up this mess.
POOF

Lousy, rotten, goofy cat . . . goin' around pretending she's a pillow . . . freaking me out . . . made me spill my lunch . . . making a big mess . . . making me get a washcloth when all I really want to do is . . .

SCREECH!

HOLY SALAMI! That goofy cat's just making things worse and worse!

I'm not sure how much more of this I can take.

I see you there pretending to be a dishrag again, ya goofy cat! Don't scream at me. Don't scream at me. Don't scream at me. Don't scream at me. Don't scream at me. Don't scream at me . . .

WHEW!

No screaming. No screaming. No screaming. No screaming. No screaming. No screaming . . .

WHEW!

You're not fooling me again, ya goofy cat. I'm grabbing this mop right here and I'm going to . . .

SCRE

ECH!

All I really wanted was to sit down, relax, have some lunch, and maybe watch a little TV.

All I really wanted was to sit down, relax, have some lunch, and maybe watch a little TV.

All I really wanted was to sit down, relax, have some lunch, and maybe watch a little TV.

All I really wanted was to sit down, relax, have some lunch, and maybe watch a little TV.

•CHAPTER THREE•

THE KITTY DIARIES

TWO MINUTES LATER . . .
NO FOOD. NO WATER.
MONSTER IS STILL
OUT THERE. IT HAS
BIG FEET.
DOG SMELLS BAD.

SIX MINUTES . . .
TWO DAYS WITHOUT FOOD. SO HUNGRY. I CAN STILL HEAR MONSTER.
DOG REALLY SMELLS BAD.

TEN MINUTES . . .
FIVE DAYS NOW. DOG STILL SMELLS BAD. DOG IS UGLY, TOO. DOG DROOLS A LOT. SO THIRSTY. MAYBE I COULD DRINK DROOL.... NO. I WOULD RATHER MONSTER EAT ME.

FIFTEEN MINUTES . . .
TRAPPED FOR OVER A WEEK NOW. I CAN'T HEAR MONSTER. DOG STILL SMELLY AND UGLY. MAYBE MONSTER WILL EAT DOG AND LEAVE ME ALONE. DOG IS STUPID.

SIXTEEN MINUTES . . .
MANY WEEKS HAVE PASSED. SO VERY, VERY HUNGRY. MUST HAVE FOOD, OR I'LL DIE! THEN MONSTER WILL FEEL SORRY. THAT'LL TEACH STUPID MONSTER. STUPID DOG.

EIGHTEEN MINUTES . . .
SO VERY, VERY, VERY HUNGRY! SMELLY, UGLY, STUPID DOG IS GONE. MONSTER MUST HAVE EATEN HIM. GOOD. BUT WHAT IS THIS?! NOW I SEE A ~~DELISHEEUS~~ ~~DEELICHIUS~~ TASTY TURKEY LEG. COULD THIS BE TRUE?

TWENTY MINUTES . . .
YES! IT'S TRUE! A TASTY, JUICY TURKEY LEG! A TURKEY LEG ALL FOR ME! I AM SO HUNGRY, AND IT IS SO TURKEY. HUNGRY. TURKEY. HUNGRY. TURKEY.

ARF!

What the . . .

SCREECH

Is she always like this around supper time?

•CHAPTER FOUR•

UNCLE MURRAY STRIKES BACK

Y'know, . . . this stuff doesn't look half bad.
KITT
PUP

All right, you two . . .

SUPPER TIME!

COME AND GET IT!

KITTY
PUPPY

GOBBLE CHEW
MUNCH MASTICATE
GNAW SLURP
GULP
CHEW
YUM
KITTY
MUNCH
EAT
GOBBLE GNAW

HEY!
BURP
KITTY
PUPPY

I HAD SHOES!

PUPPY

KITTY

PUPPY
KITTY

sigh

What's a nice dog like you doing with a goofy cat like that?
UPPY
KITTY

Oh, well . . . Let's go, dog. Why don't you help me clean this place up.

Y'know, dog . . . when I was just a kid, I had a pooch a lot like you. He was a good dog, too.

I named him Sam, and I found him lost and hungry in an alley near where I lived. He was all white except for some black spots on his face and one of his back legs.

Anyways, I still had half a sandwich on me from lunch so I tossed it to him. Boy, oh, boy was he happy to get some food into his little dog belly. You'd think he hadn't eaten anything in a year. It was just baloney, after all. No mustard, even.

I used my belt as a leash and put it around Sam's neck. At first I thought he'd go crazy when I started to pull him, but he didn't. In fact, he barked and licked my hand the whole way home.

But there was a problem. My mother wouldn't let me keep Sam in the house 'cause my baby sister was real allergic to dogs. I guess it was true, 'cause she still is. I told my mom I would keep Sam only in my room, but she told me that wouldn't really work. She was right.

So I did the only thing I could think of . . . I took little Sam to a dog shelter where they'd feed him and take good care of him.

They were real nice to Sam there. He had his own little cage, and there were lots of other dogs there for him to talk to. But the best part was that they said I could come visit him every day after school. So I did!

I went to visit Sam every single day, and each time he saw me he'd jump up and lick my face and wrestle me to the ground like he was sayin' "Gee, I'm really happy to see you! Where've you been?"

Each day, I taught him a new trick. I taught him to sit and to stay. I taught him to beg and to roll over. I even taught him geography. NAHHH! I'm just kidding about that last one. But he really was smart.

Gee, Sam and I had a lot of fun together. Then one day I walked in and didn't see him there.

A lady who worked at the shelter told me a family had come in just after I left the day before, fell in love with Sam, and took him home. She said they were real nice people and promised to feed him and take good care of him. But that didn't help. I started crying like Niagara Falls. He may not have lived with me, but Sam was MY DOG!

I thought for sure that I'd never see little Sam again.

But then, one day, about a year later, as I was walking through the park, I looked over and saw a little girl playing with a dog that looked a whole lot like my Sam. He was all white except for some black spots on his face and one of his back legs. It was him! And they were having a swell time. Sam was even doing some of the same tricks that I taught him.

It hurt me so much inside to see this little girl playing with my dog. MY DOG. But then I looked at how much fun they were having and how happy he looked, and I thought to myself . . . all I ever really wanted for that lost, hungry dog sitting alone in that alley was for someone to take him home and feed him and take good care of him. Right? And that's what I got.

I loved that dog, and now I knew that someone else loved that dog as much as me.

It was one of those days that was both real good and real bad at the same time.

Oh, well . . . Time to vacuum.
CLICK

WWWHHHHHHIIIIIRRRRRRR
SCR

ECH!
RRRRRRRRRRRRR

AUGH!
SCREECH
AUGH!
SCREECH
AUGGH!

AUGH!
CREECH!
AUGH!

UNCLE MURRAY'S FUN FACTS

WHY ARE CATS AFRAID OF VACUUM CLEANERS?

It's not the vacuum cleaner that frightens cats so much as the sudden, loud noise it makes. Most cats will react quickly to any sudden, loud noise like a car horn, or a firecracker, or someone yelling.

Cats can hear very, very well—even better than dogs. In fact, a cat can hear three times better than a human being. That's why a cat can hear a mouse rustling through the grass from 30 feet away. But it's also why loud noises are particularly painful for cats. And that's what inspires their fear.

Fear of loud noises is another survival tool for cats. If a little noise is a signal that something to eat might be nearby, then a very loud noise acts the same as a fire alarm held up next to their ears. And that means DANGER. And that means FIGHT or RUN AWAY.

When a cat is frightened, running away or hiding is a common response. But sometimes if a cat feels trapped or cornered, she'll stand still while unusual things happen to her body.

First, all of the fur on her body will stand on end. Then the cat will arch her back up using all sixty of her vertebrae—humans have only thirty-four, by the way. This will make the cat look much bigger; a tactic it uses to intimidate its enemies. But the sign to be very aware of is when a cat has turned its ears back. A cat will do this when it feels like fighting back and wants to protect those sensitive ears. That is a clear sign to back away from a VERY angry cat that could attack you.

Never mind all that ear stuff! I gotta go grab that cat!

SCREE

Here,
Kitty,
Kitty,
Kitty!

•CHAPTER FIVE•

CATCH THAT KITTY

*Hark!

SCREECH!

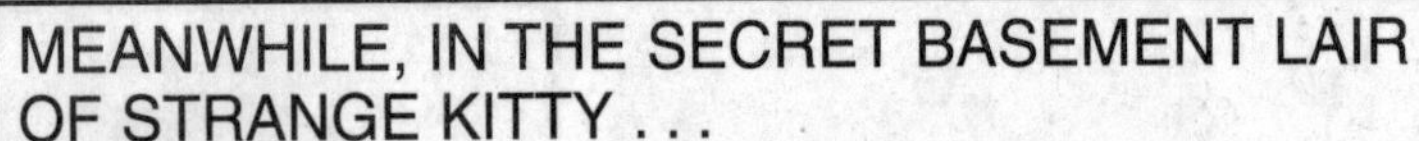
MEANWHILE, IN THE SECRET BASEMENT LAIR OF STRANGE KITTY . . .

DO YOU HEAR THAT, OLD CHUM? I DO BELIEVE I HEAR PLAINTIVE CRIES FOR HELP FROM OUR OLD FELINE FRIEND WITH THE BLACK FUR AND REBELLIOUS ATTITUDE!
BIG COMIC OF ROBOTS

HOLY CATNIP, S.K.! WE CAN'T IGNORE A PLAINTIVE CRY FOR HELP!

RIGHT YOU ARE, OLD BEAN! ONCE AGAIN, THE WORLD IS IN NEED OF . . .

FANTASTIC CAT
AND POWER MOUSE
THE RODENT WONDER

Fc

OKAY . . . LET'S SEE HERE . . .
COOL UTILITY BELT?
YUP!

SUPER COOL MYSTICAL CAPE OF NINJA STEALTH?
YUP!

SUPER, HYPER COOL FLASHLIGHT WITH COPYRIGHT-PROTECTED LOGO TAPED ON IT?
YUP!

SPATULA?
YUP!

OKEY DOKEY!
LET'S GO!

WAIT!
WHAT'S WRONG?

WE NEED A BETTER CALL-TO-ACTION SHOUT THAN "OKEY DOKEY."
YOU'RE RIGHT. HMMM . . .

HOW ABOUT . . .
"UP, UP, AND AWAY!"
IT'S BEEN DONE.

"ON YOUR MARK, GET SET, GO!"
IT DOESN'T FEEL QUITE RIGHT.

"I'M DREAMING OF A WHITE CHRISTMAS!"
TOO SEASONAL.

CHEESE POPCORN?
HMMM . . . WILL IT REALLY STRIKE FEAR IN THE HEARTS OF OUR MOST BITTER AND DANGEROUS ENEMIES?

NO . . . I MEAN . . . I'M GOING TO MAKE SOME CHEESE POPCORN. DO YOU WANT SOME?
OH, I SEE. YES, PLEASE.

WAIT! I'VE GOT IT!
REALLY?

LOOK OUT FOR THE SPATULA!
I LOVE IT!

OH, GOOD! THEN IT'S SETTLED . . .

LOOK OUT FOR
THE SPATULA!
WOW! THIS IS REALLY GOOD POPCORN!
FC

•CHAPTER SIX•

KITTIES TO THE RESCUE

Almost . . . almost . . .
Hey! How come you look bigger all of a sudden?
HISSSS!

GOTCHA!
SCREECH!

What's happening?

YIKES!
HISS
SPIT

HOLY SALAMI! That goofy cat's suddenly turned into a biting, spitting hurricane of fur and claws!

EEE
GNARL!
SPI
HISS!

EEEEEEK!
MEOW!

EEEEEK!

GRRRR!
FFT!
SNARL!

SLAM!

Well . . .
at least I
got her back
in the house.

KNOCK
KNOCK
Who's there?

MEOW!
"Meow" who?

*Let us in, and I mean RIGHT MEOW!

HOLY SALAMI!
Is the entire world full of goofy cats?!

MEOW
MEOW

Boy-oh-boy-oh-boy! This day just can't get any weirder.

LOOK OUT FOR THE SPATULA!
Huh?
FC

WHAP
WHAP
WHAPPITY
WHAP!
GET OFFA ME! GET OFFA ME!

EEEEEEEE
WHAP
WHAP
WHAP

EE
EEEEE

EEEEEEEE
MEOW
MEOW

EEEEEEEEEEK!

THAT'S ENOUGH

WHOA!

I want all of you goofy cats out of this house RIGHT MEOW . . . I mean . . .

RIGHT NOW!!

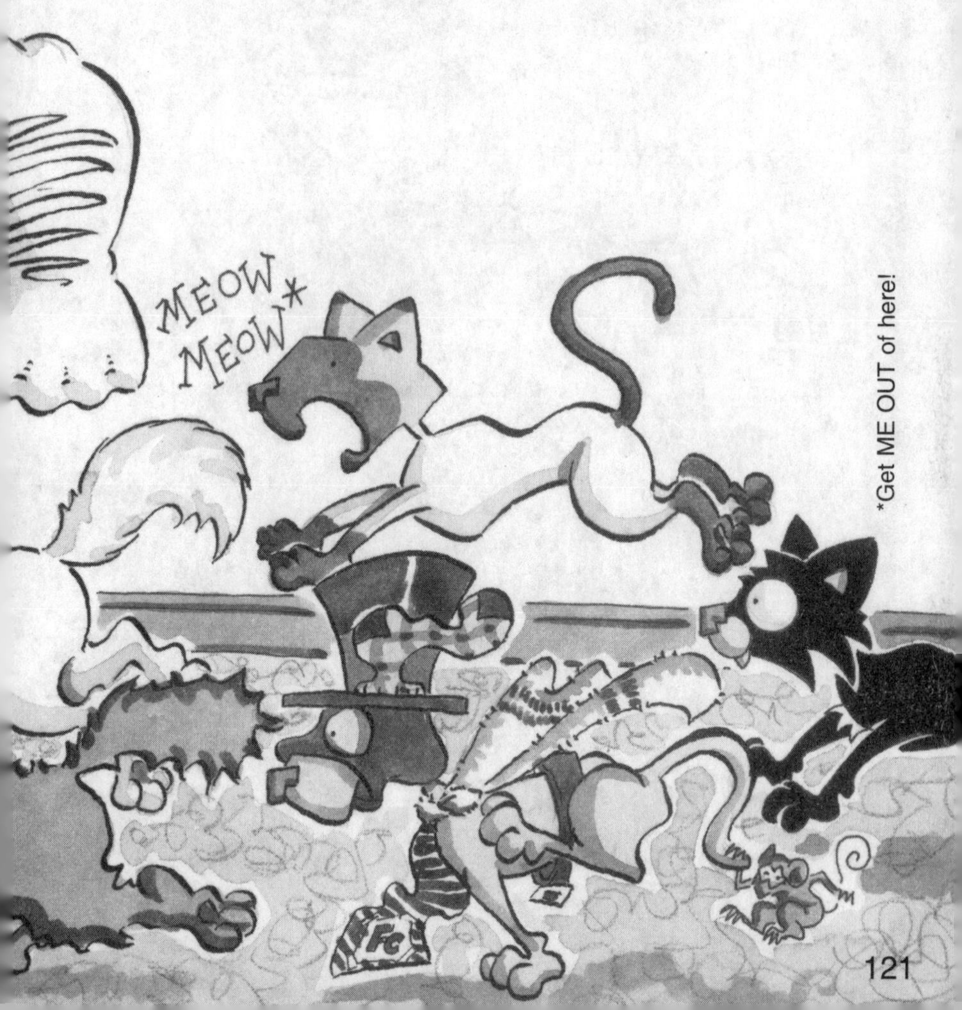
MEOW MEOW*
*Get ME OUT of here!

SLAM
NOT YOU!

NOOOOOOOOOO!
NOT YOU! You don't get to leave! Why? Because I'M the one that's leaving!

That's right! You heard me! As soon as I open this door, I'll be free. FREE! No more goofy cats screaming in my face and eating my shoes. No more biting and scratching and chasing me down the street. Outside this door is a big, wonderful world where goofy cats don't turn into furry whirlwinds that hit me on the head with a spatula. And soon I will be a part of that world once again!
YAWN

I don't know why you hate me, cat, because I'm a real nice guy. I've got friends who like me and a family who loves me. And I got feelings that you're always hurting. So that's why I'M LEAVING!

SLAM

AND I'M TAKING THE DOG WITH ME! WHY? BECAUSE HE'S A GOOD DOGGIE! AND YOU'RE NOT!

HE'S A GOOD BOY! AND YOU'RE A BAD KITTY!
GOOD BOY! BAD KITTY! GOOD BOY! BAD KITTY! GOOD BOY! BAD KITTY!

SLAM!

GOODBYE,
BAD KITTY!

•CHAPTER SEVEN•

KITTY ON HER OWN

MEOW?

UNCLE MURRAY'S FUN FACTS

WHY ARE SOME CATS AFRAID OF BEING ALONE?

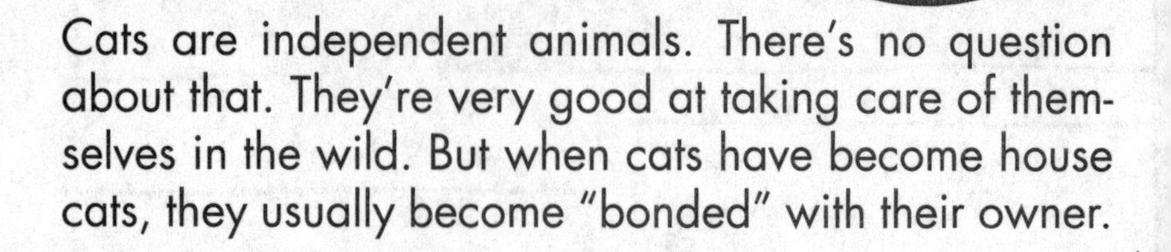

Cats are independent animals. There's no question about that. They're very good at taking care of themselves in the wild. But when cats have become house cats, they usually become "bonded" with their owner.

When a cat becomes very close, even dependent on a human being for food or protection, that's called "bonding."

And sometimes when that bond is broken, even for just a little while, some cats might exhibit "separation anxiety." Have you ever seen a baby begin to cry just because her Mommy has left the room for just a few seconds? That's a good example of "separation anxiety," and even cats can get it.

Leave cats alone for too long and they'll start to cry out to see if anyone is in the house, just like a baby. Sometimes they'll even lose their appetite and not

eat. The most anxious cats will even pull out clumps of their own fur because of nervousness.

The solution for all fears is to let the cat gradually grow used to whatever scares them. Cats can adapt very quickly.

If a cat is afraid of people, keep your distance and step a little closer day by day while also letting her come to you under her own power. If your cat is afraid of loud noises, try to keep the sound down at first if possible, and then increase the exposure a little bit each day.

And if the cat is afraid of being alone, give her time to adjust as she learns that you'll eventually return. She'll hate being alone at first, but in time she'll learn that there's nothing to be afraid of once you keep coming back.

MEOW

MEOW!

MEOW
MEOW
MEOW

MEOW

Hi.
I'm back.
ME...

I made a promise to feed you all week and take good care of you all week. And I'm going to keep that promise even if you act mean and goofy to me all week.

So, let's you and me make a deal, cat. We're going to be stuck together for the next few days. I'm going to feed you and take good care of you no matter what.
And in return . . . how about you be just a little nicer to me.

So, what do you say, ya goofy cat?
Do we have a deal?

PURR?

PURR.

Well, okay then.
That turned out to be easier than I thought.

MEOW
CRASH
BLAM
WOOF
Although . . . something tells me this is STILL going to be a very long week.
THUMP
ARF
HISS
KA-BOOM
DING
SPLAT

• EPILOGUE •

ONE WEEK LATER . . .

WE'RE BACK!

WOOF
WOOF WOOF
WOOF

Thank you so much, Uncle Murray, for taking such good care of Kitty and Puppy. I know they can be a real handful. I hope they weren't too much trouble.

What did you say, Uncle Murray?

Fish don't bite or scream or chase you around the house or hit you on the head with a spatula. All they do is swim around and make nice little bubbles that don't hurt anybody. And they're pretty. Pretty like little rainbows. Fish.
Fish don't bite or scream or chase you around the house or . . .

Hmmm . . . Oh, well. Goodbye, Uncle Murray. And thanks again.

HI, KITTY!
Did you miss us?

Awwww! We missed you, too, Kitty!

HEY! Do you remember that REAL BIG SURPRISE we promised you? Do you? DO YOU?!

Well, here she is!

To be continued . . .

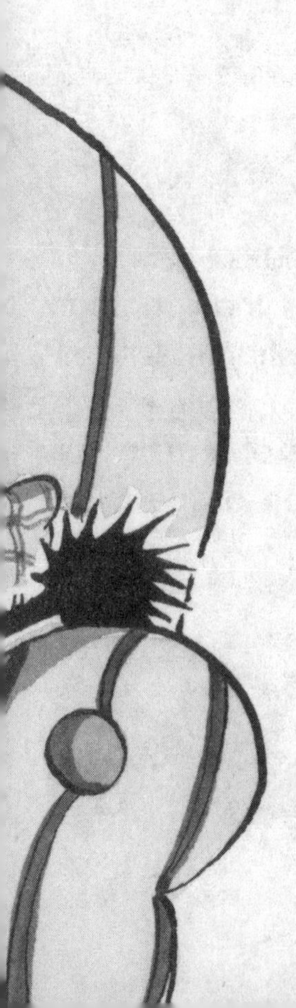

• APPENDIX •

A SELECTION OF PHOBIAS

A "phobia" is a strong fear of a specific object or a specific situation. Most of the time the fear is irrational, meaning that the person who has the phobia really has nothing to fear. For instance, a boy might be afraid of worms (Scoleciphobia), but that doesn't mean the boy has any real reason to be afraid of worms, other than he thinks they're scary and doesn't want them anywhere near him.

Ten percent of the people who live in the United States have a phobia. That's over thirty million people! This means that phobias are very common and nothing to be ashamed of.

We've seen a lot of different examples of fear in this book. The following is a small selection of the more than five hundred known phobias.

Agrizoophobia—Fear of wild animals.

Ailurophobia (also, Elurophobia)—Fear of cats.

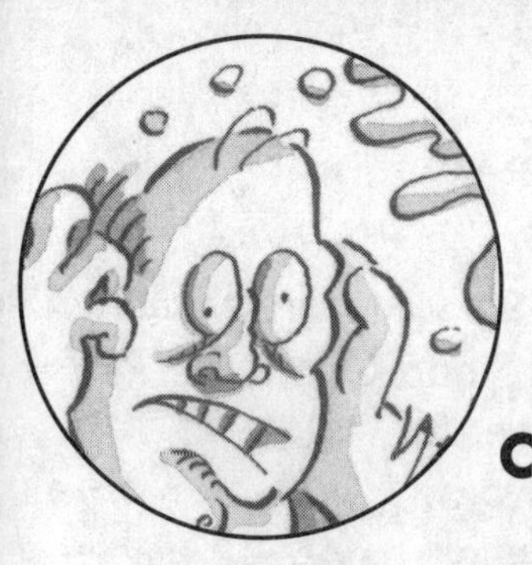

Amychophobia—Fear of scratches or being scratched.

Cynophobia—Fear of dogs.

Ligyrophobia (also, Phonophobia)—Fear of loud noises, also, fear of voices or one's own voice.

Lilapsophobia—Fear of hurricanes or tornadoes.

Monophobia (also Autophobia)—Fear of being alone.

Olfactophobia (also, Osmophobia)—Fear of smells or odors.

Peladophobia—Fear of bald people.

Phagophobia—Fear of swallowing, eating, or being eaten.

Pnigophobia—Fear of being choked or smothered.

Teratophobia—Fear of monsters.

• ABOUT THE AUTHOR •

NICK BRUEL has written and illustrated some pretty funny books, including *Poor Puppy*, *Boing*, *Bob and Otto*, *Little Red Bird*, and *Who is Melvin Bubble?*, winner of the North Carolina Children's Choice Award. HOWEVER, he is probably best known as the author of the Tennessee, Wyoming, and Indiana Children's Choice Award winner *Bad Kitty* (available in regular and special Cat-Nipped editions), about which some very important people said:

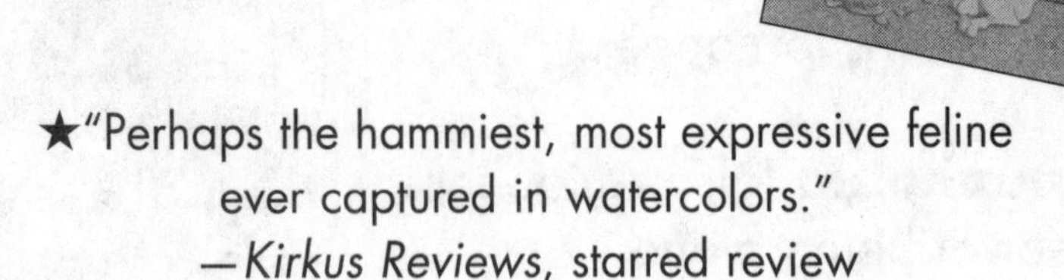

★"Perhaps the hammiest, most expressive feline ever captured in watercolors."
—*Kirkus Reviews*, starred review

★"Will have youngsters howling with laughter."
—*Publishers Weekly*, starred review

He is also infamous for his Bad Kitty chapter books, *Bad Kitty Gets a Bath* (winner of a 2009 Gryphon Honor), and *Happy Birthday, Bad Kitty*. Visit him online at www.nickbruel.com.

Little did Kitty know that soon there would be another.

Almost.

Life was not as it once was, but eventually it became good again.

Over time, Kitty became used to life with the beast. Even its horrible odor became tolerable. The brave Kitty had found areas of shelter where she could evade the beast and its terrible liquid.

At times, though she would never admit it, she became almost fond of the beast.

Kitty fought bravely to rid her once peaceful kingdom of the cruel beast. But even she wasn't mighty enough to defeat the evil creature.

A foul and wretched beast had arrived as if from nowhere.

Its face was deformed and grotesque. Its massive black nose was always cold and always wet. Its breath was so hot and so foul that its odor could mask the stench of a hundred dead fish lying in the sun. And it seemed to be filled with a noxious, clear liquid that continuously dripped out of the vast, gaping maw it called its mouth.

. . . the skies became dark, the ground began to shake, the air became cold and dank and filled with a horrible stench.

The years passed, and Kitty was happy to eat alone, play alone, and sleep alone. Life continued to be good—alone.

BUT ONE DAY . . .

Kitty ate her food—alone.

Kitty played with her toys—alone.

Kitty slept on the sofa—alone.

IN THE BEGINNING, THERE WAS KITTY.

Just Kitty.

Only Kitty.

Kitty—all by herself.

And life was good.

DING-
DONG!

MEOW MEOW HISS

SPIT MEOW

HISS MEOW FFT

FFT HISS MEOW

MEOW SPIT FFT

MEOW HISS

•INTRODUCTION•

IN THE BEGINNING

Kitty has spent years getting used to Puppy. Now she's got something even more diabolical to deal with.

Bad Kitty's shenanigans continue in

Bad Kitty Meets the Baby

"blocked," it's because you DO have something in mind that you want to put to paper, but you don't feel it's good enough for what you're trying to accomplish. That's the pride part. The best thing, I find, is to put it down anyways and move on. Half the challenge of the writing process is the self-editing process.

What would you do if you ever stopped writing?
I would seriously consider becoming a teacher.

What do you like best about yourself?
I have nice hands. They've always served me well.

What is your worst habit?
Biting other people's toenails.

What do you consider to be your greatest accomplishment?
Adopting our spectacular daughter, Isabel. Actually managing to get my first book (*Boing!*) published comes in second.

Where in the world do you feel most at home?
Home. I'm a homebody. I like to work at home. I like to cook at home. I like to grow my garden vegetables at home. I like being in new and different places, but I despise the process of getting there. So, because I'm not a big fan of traveling, I just like being at HOME. It's a quality about myself that runs closely with my love of solitude.

What do you wish you could do better?
I wish I was a better artist. I look at the fluidity of line and the luminous colors of paintings by such artists as Ted Lewin, Anik McGrory, Jerry Pinkney, and Arthur Rackham with complete awe.

What are you most afraid of?
Scorpions. ACK! They're like the creepiest parts of spiders and crabs smashed together into one nasty-looking character. Who's idea was that?

What time of year do you like best?
Spring and summer.

What's your favorite TV show?
I have to give my propers to *The Simpsons,* of course. But I'm very partial to the British mystery series *Lovejoy.*

If you were stranded on a desert island, who would you want for company?
I'm going to defy the implications of that question and say no one. As much as I'm comfortable talking for hours with any number of people, I'm also one of those people who relishes solitude. I've never had any problem with being alone for long periods of time. . . . You get a lot more work done that way.

If you could travel in time, where would you go?
America in the 1920's. All of my favorite literature, movies, and music comes from that period. I would love to have witnessed or even participated in the artistic movements of that period in history.

What's the best advice you have ever received about writing?
I had a playwriting teacher in college named Bob Butman who gave me superb advice on the subject of writer's block—it's all about PRIDE. It's a complete myth to believe that you can't think about what you want to write next because your mind is a blank. In truth, when you feel

Are you a morning person or a night owl?
Both. I suspect that I need less sleep than most people. I'm usually the first one up to make breakfast. And I'm rarely in bed before 11:00 PM. Maybe this is why I'm exhausted all the time.

What's your idea of the best meal ever?
So long as it's Chinese food, I don't care. I just love eating it. If I had to pick a favorite dish, it would be Duck Chow Fun, which I can only find in a few seedy diners in Chinatown.

Which do you like better: cats or dogs?
Oh, I know everyone is going to expect me to say cats, but in all honesty, I love them both.

What do you value most in your friends?
Sense of humor and reliability.

Where do you go for peace and quiet?
I'm the father of a one-year-old. What is this "peez kwiet" thing you speak of?

What makes you laugh out loud?
The Marx Brothers. W. C. Fields. Buster Keaton. And my daughter.

What's your favorite song?
I don't think I have one favorite song, but "If You Want to Sing Out, Sing Out" by Cat Stevens comes to mind.

Who is your favorite fictional character?
The original Captain Marvel. He's the kind of superhero designed for kids who need superheroes. SHAZAM!

Where do you write your books?

As I write this, I'm the father of a one-year-old baby. Because of all the attention she needs, I've developed a recent habit, when the babysitter comes by to watch Isabel, of collecting all of my work together and bringing it all to a nice little Chinese restaurant across the street called A Taste of China. They know me pretty well, and let me sit at one of their tables for hours while I nibble on a lunch special.

Where do you find inspiration for your writing?

Other books. The only true axiom to creative expression is that to be productive at what you do, you have to pay attention to what everyone else is doing. I think this is true for writing, for painting, for playing music, for anything that requires any sort of creative output. To put it more simply for my situation . . . if you want to write books, you have to read as many books as you can.

Which of your characters is most like you?

In *Happy Birthday, Bad Kitty*, I introduce a character named Strange Kitty. I can say without any hesitation that Strange Kitty is me as a child. I was definitely the cat who would go to a birthday party and spend the entire time sitting in the corner reading comic books rather than participating in all of the pussycat games.

When you finish a book, who reads it first?

My wife, Carina. Even if I'm on a tight deadline, she'll see it first before I even send it to my editor, Neal Porter. Carina has a fine sense of taste for the work I do. I greatly respect her opinion even when she's a little more honest than I'd like her to be.

What's your most embarrassing childhood memory?
Crying my eyes out while curled up in my cubbyhole in first grade for reasons I can't remember. I didn't come back out until my mother came in to pick me up from school.

What's your favorite childhood memory?
Waking up early on Christmas morning to see what Santa brought me.

As a young person, who did you look up to most?
My father. He was a kind man with a great sense of humor.

What was your worst subject in school?
True story: In eighth grade, I was on the second string of the B-Team of middle school baseball. I was up at bat only twice the entire season. I struck out and was beaned. It was generally recognized that I was the worst player on the team. And since our team lost every single game it played that year, it was decided that I was probably the worst baseball player in all of New York State in 1978.

What was your best subject in school?
Art, with English coming in a close second.

What was your first job?
I spent most of the summer after my junior year in college as an arts and crafts director at a camp for kids with visual disabilities in Central Florida. I won't say any more, because I'm likely to write a book about it someday.

How did you celebrate publishing your first book?
I honestly don't remember. A lot was happening at that time. When *Boing!* came out, I was also preparing to get married. Plus, I was hard at work on *Bad Kitty*.

GOFISH

questions for the author

NICK BRUEL

What did you want to be when you grew up?
I tell this story all the time when I visit schools. When I was in first grade, there was nothing I liked to do more than to write stories and make little drawings to go with them. I thought the best job in the world was the one held by those people who had the comic strips in the newspapers. What better job is there than to wake up each morning and spend the day writing little stories and making little drawings to go along with them. So that's what I did. I wrote stories and I drew pictures to go along with them. And I still do that to this day.

When did you realize you wanted to be a writer?
I always liked to write stories. But it wasn't until high school when I spent a lot of time during summer vacations writing plays for my own amusement that I began to think this was something I could do as a career.

What's your first childhood memory?
Sitting in my high chair feeling outraged that my parents were eating steak and green beans while all I had was a bowl of indescribable mush.